TIGER TROUBLE

ALASKAN TIGERS: BOOK TWELVE

MARISSA DOBSON

Published by Dobson Ink
Printed in the United States of America
ISBN-13: 978-1-946474-05-6

Dedication:

To my readers: Thank you for your support and for loving the Alaskan Tigers series as much as I do. Tex's book was somewhat unexpected. He wasn't supposed to get his story until later, but Tex wanted to show everyone that he's a different man. He wanted everyone to know that the Texas Tigers would not be defeated by what happened to them. They would come out stronger than ever. This is just a hint of what their future will be like.

Chapter One

The Texas Tigers had been growing stronger with each passing day and their scars were fading. It had been an uphill struggle, but little by little, Tex was uniting the clan and slowly abolishing Avery from every corner of Manetka Resort. That's why he was in Alaska. This trip would assist him when it came to steering the clan in the right direction.

Sitting in the balcony of the new training center, he was amazed by the work that'd been completed in the months since he had left. The new building housed everything the guards needed for their training, with the biggest area being the main gym—an open space with mats allowing for softer takedowns when practicing hand-to-hand combat. The balcony had been added so that the Alpha or trainers could watch without those below realizing they were being observed. His gaze scanned each of the guards as they partook in the practice fight, watching them closely to see how they handled themselves, while his thoughts circled around the clan. The journey before them was long and there would be obstacles they'd have to overcome before they'd remotely resemble a normal clan. They had been stifled for so long that they needed to learn to breathe again. Most of them weren't psychologically or physically able to protect the resort yet. The damage caused by the former abusive Alpha—Avery—would need to be repaired over time.

If he wanted to keep his clan safe, he had to add strong members. Too many of his people were broken. For years, they'd been controlled until they had no will of their own. They were starting to realize that Tex wouldn't treat them the way Avery had. For the first time, they were free to live their lives again. They didn't have to worry about being abused for speaking their minds. However, like any Alpha, he still had the final say, and they needed to understand he had their best interests at heart.

Shifting slightly on the metal folding chair, he leaned forward and forced himself to focus on the action below him. Thinking about the clan and all the work ahead of them wouldn't help him decide which guards would be the best to take back to Texas. They needed guards—actual guards who could protect them. He had a few, but not enough he trusted completely to protect his Lieutenant, Ben, and the rest of the clan.

"For his size, I'm surprised."

Tex didn't have to look at Rhett to know which guard he was talking about. He shifted his gaze away from Milo, who'd been sparring with another potential guard, and focused on what appeared at first glance a mismatched pair. Brody and Taber. At five-foot-six, Brody was the shortest candidate, yet he'd gone up against the Kodiak Bear, Taber.

"When they squared off, I somewhat discounted him," Rhett said. "He doesn't appear to be much of a threat."

"Which is what we need. A surprise."

That could work both ways. If someone underestimated Brody, it could mean safety issues for whomever he was guarding, but he was a strong possibility. This was why Tex had brought Rhett with him. As an Elder Guard, his priority was protecting Tex and Ben, while unofficially he'd become a trusted advisor to both men. Rhett was assigned as the Captain of Tex's Guards, but whenever Ben left the resort, Rhett went along, assuming Tex wasn't headed out on a mission. They needed more guards like him, not only for the Elder Guards but also to protect the members, resort, and the guests. Without more like him, the clan was at risk. With Manetka Resort scheduled to open in a few weeks, he needed to ensure he could protect his clan.

He'd been looking forward to the trip, hoping to catch up with friends he'd made during his time there. In the hours he'd been there, however, he'd only become more agitated. He was worried they wouldn't find the guards they needed. He kept wondering what was happening back in Texas, and what the future would hold. Being in Alaska reminded him of how quickly things changed. Since he had left, they added the guards' indoor training arena with viewing balcony, and the second floor Elders quarters would be finished in a few weeks. Time stood still for no one, but part of him missed the life he'd had here.

When Ben nominated him as Alpha of the Texas Tigers, he hadn't thought twice. They needed him, and there was work to be done. He took the position without realizing it meant giving up what meant so much to him. The morning coffee chats he shared with Robin, and occasionally Harmony, had been times he'd treasured. Both women were happily mated, but he hadn't been interested in them that way. The friendship they developed was important to him, and now, sitting in the guards' training arena, he realized just how much he missed that.

Tex took his white cowboy hat off and dropped it on the seat next to him. The guards he'd been considering were all committed to Tabitha and her uniting the tiger shifters, leaving one less thing for him to worry about, but bringing in outsiders would be a challenge. How would his clan members react? Even the vetting he planned to do of those coming to Manetka wouldn't eliminate every possible issue. All the more reason to have capable guards.

"What do you think?" he asked.

Minutes ticked by as he waited for Rhett to answer, allowing him time to continue reminding himself why he was there and why this was so important. He watched the guards closely as Styx, Milo, and Taber put them through their paces.

"Ty picked some good possibilities for you." Rhett glanced down at the e-tablet he had in his hand, assessing each of the candidates participating in the training session.

Knowing there was more to that statement, he turned to Rhett and assessed his most trusted guard. Even though he had been through Hell with the rest of the Texas Tigers, Rhett came out better than most. His scars were minimal but the changes in him were astronomical as he embraced his freedom and his new role.

"But?" Tex asked when the guard remained silent.

"Dawson and Brody are my top choices." He gave Tex a moment to find them in the group. "Dawson has a way of anticipating his opponent's next move and being ready for it. If he can't move out of the way, he blocks it. Brody's like a boxer. He stays on the balls of his feet. This is allowing him to compensate for his size, giving him the ability to spring in any direction. An unknown opponent would discount him as a threat and believe he'd be easy to take down. His flexibility gives him an advantage. He's a street fighter and he does it dirty. While others with martial arts training might take him down quicker, Brody's going to do the most damage."

"Going against Taber could have worked against him, but somehow he made taking on the bear look as if they were on a level playing field. Taber's not only taller and outweighs him, but his arms are longer, so Brody has to get into his striking zone in order to hit him." Tex turned from Brody and Taber, focusing on Milo and the candidate he was working with. "What about Thorn?"

"He's got skills but needs polish." Rhett tapped Thorn's picture, bringing up his profile. "He's formerly of the Mississippi Tigers. He left after his Alpha refused to commit to Tabitha."

"The Mississippi Tigers are going to be a problem. I'm not sure Ty knows how to deal with them, but he's going to have to deal with Lee sooner rather than later." His gaze remained on Thorn as the man's fist slammed into Milo's shoulder.

In a fight, it was smart to go after the opponent's weakness, but Thorn didn't seem to realize it would only enrage Milo further. His injured shoulder kept him out of the field for too long. Even now he had to deal with the pain that came with it. When a shifter was injured, they could normally shift and heal, but Milo didn't have the opportunity when the rouge sliced through his shoulder, severing some of the nerve endings and muscles. As an Elder Guard, he couldn't allow a weakness to permit his enemy to overcome him during a fight, so he fought through it and the pain turned into fury. Which landed Thorn flat on back on the practice mat.

"We could have an issue with Thorn." Rhett held the tablet out to him. "His sister is here, as well, and he's seeking a clan for both of them."

"It's doable." He scanned the file but it didn't say anything more about the sister. "We're meeting with each of the guards individually after they've showered and changed. If he's still on the short list after we've spoken with him, we'll meet with her, too. If we choose him, they'll both have to make the commitment to me as their Alpha."

"I'd like to work with whoever makes the short list separately before you offer them the opportunity to serve you. I want to test their skills myself."

That was another reason Rhett was their top man. Not only was he willing to speak his mind, but he thought things through. The clan meant as much to him as it meant to Tex and Ben. "We'll arrange it for tomorrow.

Today's going to be long enough without adding to your schedule. You decide the order, but let's not alert them. I don't want to give them the opportunity to prepare for it. I want to know what they'll be like if they're caught off guard."

"I know you're hoping to add at least one Elder Guard out of this group. I suggest anyone you're considering gets an extra dose of surprise."

"What are you thinking?" He raised an eyebrow at Rhett, wondering if he had a devious plan in mind.

"We'll call on the one you're interested in during the night. Wake them up and see how they manage. Lack of sleep is something Elder Guards have to deal with at times and this will give us a chance to see if he can handle it. If there's more than one, we'll do them back to back so they can't alert the others."

"Better yet, if they speak about what happened they'll be eliminated from the running." A whistle blew, letting the potential guards know the session was over. "Only those who get through the session, as well as the Alaskan Tigers Elders, will know what we're up to."

"Considering our short time frame, it will be the best way to give us insight into how they function under pressure. Bringing a new team in is going to be hard enough, but if they don't work out, it's going to be for nothing." Rhett hit the power button on the tablet, darkening the screen, and stood. "My Queen."

"I'll never get used to being addressed like that." Tabitha smiled as she came to stand in front of them, with Felix beside her. "Ty's attending to something, but I wanted to find out how things went. Did any of the possibilities match what you were looking for?"

"Your mate once again amazed me. He picked some worthy candidates." He rose from where he had been sitting and smiled at Tabitha. It had only been a few weeks since he had seen her last, but it seemed like so much longer. He owed a lot to her and Robin. They'd brought him out of his depression, given him the strength to continue, and encouraged him when they learned he wanted to be part of the group that took Avery down. More than that, they became his first true friends and showed him it was possible to trust someone. They would be there when he needed them, just as he'd be there for them.

"Wonderful. Styx and the others have been working them hard since they arrived, trying to get them in shape to do the job you need them to do. He has preferences as to who would be able to handle protecting you and Ben, but all of them are capable of being ground guards."

"I wouldn't expect anything less. I know you understand the challenges for our species, as well as what I'm facing with the Texas Tigers and Manetka Resort."

"Opening the resort with some of the members living on the top floors is going to create an additional challenge for you and your team, but I know you can handle it. You have to trust yourself and those you've surrounded yourself with. If you ever run into any issues, you know we're all behind you." Tabitha placed her hand on his arm, giving it a light squeeze. "Have Jinx's men finished the security measures?"

"Keycard doors are being installed now for all of the suites. Larry installed the passcode doors to the floors the clan will use and the elevators will be coded to access those floors, as well. There are security cameras covering every aspect of the public areas of the resort. The clan areas have cameras in the hall to ensure there are no unauthorized persons on the floor, but that's it," Rhett explained. "I've sat down with Ben, Barry, and Larry numerous times to go over the security measures. I'm confident that we're doing everything we can in that area to ensure the safety of the Elders and the clan. What we're lacking are additional guards. Hopefully, this trip will help us secure that, as well."

"I hope so." Tabitha nodded.

"Why don't we go to the conference room?" Felix suggested.

"There's someone waiting to see you, Tex." Tabitha smiled, her eyes glistening with amusement. "Ty will join us shortly. The potential guards will be brought in one by one, as they're ready, unless you have an order you'd like to see them in."

"No. Whoever is showered and ready first is fine. The conference room would be great. We have something to discuss in private with you and Ty, anyway." Tex waited for her to lead the way as eagerness rose within him. He wasn't sure who was waiting for him, but he had no enemies at the clan. It must be someone he knew—a reunion with an old friend, perhaps?

Lingering in the back, hidden in the shadows, Carleen watched as Thorn fought against Milo. He was working so hard, doing his best to make the guard team for the Alpha who was visiting. The Alpha of the Texas Tigers wasn't the only one who would come to inspect the potential guards, but for some reason her brother wanted to impress him more than the others. He wanted to be chosen for Texas but she couldn't understand why. They were from Mississippi, so coming to Alaska had been a huge shock to her system. Now that she was there, she loved it. She loved the snow. The fluffy white stuff cooled under the pads of her paws and when she rolled in it, white dust floated around her. It was even more beautiful to watch as it fell.

She knew they couldn't stay there, but she'd hoped they could live in a climate that had snow. The Ohio Tigers' Alpha had been looking for additional guards, and so were the Connecticut Tigers. This wasn't the only opportunity but she hadn't been able to convince Thorn of that.

It was wrong of her to sit there and watch, hoping he'd mess up. Some little thing that wouldn't put him out of the running completely, but might cause this Alpha to turn him down. Hoping for him to screw up made her feel horrible. He was her brother and they'd been through everything together. The thought of her wanting him to fail was wrong, yet she hadn't been able to stop herself from wishing until she saw *him*.

There was no doubt in her mind the man holding her attention was the visiting Alpha from the Texas Tigers. He watched the men in the fight session with such intensity, but he didn't seem to notice her. Staying hidden in the shadows, she observed him. The authority pouring off him made him stand out against the other man sitting beside him. He wasn't big and muscular like she expected from an Alpha. His body was lean and toned. The contours of the muscles in his arms were well-defined, making her want to run her tongue along them.

What the hell? She shook her head at the very thought, but the image of him lying naked on a bed, only a sheet draped over his waist, lingered in her thoughts. She could see herself crouched over him, kissing his body, feeling his hard muscles under her fingers as she leaned forward to drag her tongue along the contours of his arms. As if he could feel her fantasy, he turned to look at her and their gazes locked. *Shit.*

This wasn't normal for her. She never had thoughts like this about someone and it unnerved her. She barely noticed the whistle when it blew, ending the session and allowing Thorn and the others to head to the showers. She needed to get away and clear her mind. Forcing herself to tear her gaze away from the visiting Alpha, she scurried off in the direction from which she'd come. Desperate to escape, she ran down the steps. The safety of the two-bedroom cabin she shared with her brother was her only security.

She couldn't allow herself to feel this way toward anyone when her life was so uncertain. Fantasies might be a way to escape the pressures of the indefinite future, but she couldn't afford to focus on one man, especially not an Alpha. There was too much at stake.

Racing back to the cabin, her brother's words echoed through her mind: *Alphas are off limits, Carleen. Don't ever forget what happened to Lucy.*

Chapter Two

Even though the second floor was being added to the main building, everything else remained the same. It almost made Tex feel at home as Tabitha led him to the conference room with no windows. While there were two, this was the one most used by the Elders because of the location. It gave them additional protection. The walls were a cheerful yellow, giving a light and airy feel, but it was seeing Robin sitting at the table that drew a smile to his lips.

"Well, it seems being an Alpha suits you." She rose from the table and came to him with her arms spread, ready for a hug.

"You won't believe it, but I'm not half bad at this." He wrapped his arms around her, squeezing her tighter than usual, as if that would make it last. "You should come see all the changes with the clan."

"I knew you could do it." She returned his squeeze and they separated.

"Does that mean we're invited back?" Adam stepped into the room.

Rhett's sudden movement from his side caused Tex to push Robin behind him, using his body to shield her from whatever danger Rhett had sensed as he turned toward the doorway. It quickly became clear there was no danger, but why had Rhett reacted?

"Hey now…" Adam sized him up, clearly ready to tear his throat out for blocking his way to his mate—Robin.

"Rhett." Tex had never seen him overreact, and he needed to rein it in.

"Adam's my mate," Robin explained, as Ty stepped in, directly behind

Adam. "He's no threat to you or Tex."

"Easy. Everything is fine." Tex could see Rhett's unease but before he could do anything about it, Ty came farther into the room, heading directly past them as he made his way to Tabitha.

"Your first time on duty protecting an Elder can be a challenge, Rhett. Especially surrounded by another clan and outnumbered," Ty said, while standing next to his mate. Felix remained close to her opposite side. "You're uneasy and that's to be expected, but you'll find no threats here. We would never harm you or your Alpha. Tex is not only our ally and our friend, he's family."

"I apologize." Rhett's gaze landed on Ty. "This is your home and I never meant to imply you weren't keeping your clan safe."

"Another Alpha might jump to that conclusion, but I know what happened in Texas. You're not...how should I put it? As socialized as other guards might be. So far, you've mostly had to protect the Elders from people who've come to you and you know they're on our sides, which takes some of the worry out of your job. It's always easier to defend your Elders on your own land than it is when you're visiting another clan."

"But he knows we're committed," Robin reasoned. "Everyone here has committed themselves to you and to Tabitha's goals."

"True, but it's still overwhelming for him. Adam..." Ty nodded to him as if giving him permission for something, but Tex wasn't sure what.

Adam shut the door to the conference room and stepped closer to Rhett. "Take a deep breath. What do you smell?"

A growl echoed the space and when Tex reached out for his guard, Ty shook his head, stopping him.

"Stand down, Rhett. That's an order." Tex trusted Rhett, but the change in his stance caused him to issue a command. He glanced back at Ty. "What's going on?"

"You're used to it, so you're not alarmed, but your guard isn't accustomed," Ty explained. "Adam's arrival brought a scent that alarmed him. It put him on edge, even if he didn't realize it."

"It's Daisy." Tabitha shook her head, sending a strand of her strawberry blonde hair falling from her hair clip. "I should have warned you, but I hadn't considered that her scent would alarm him like this."

"She's a threat." Rhett snarled.

"She's been here weeks and while she's not committed to the clan, I can ensure you she's not going to cause any problems," Ty explained. "She was kept prisoner by Pierce and is—"

"Unstable," Adam supplied.

"Anyone who's gone through what she has would be." Robin stepped back to the chair she had vacated and sank into it. "She's gone through Hell and I tried to work with her but she's not ready to move past it. As much as she doesn't want to continue to relive the past, she's unwilling to let it go. Every time we take a step in the right direction, it seems we lose momentum. She's not moving backward, but she's unable to move forward for days...sometimes longer."

"Daisy is guarded. She's not leaving her cabin, but even if she did, there are too many guards stationed around the grounds for her to get this far." Adam stepped past Rhett and went to his mate, Robin. "Either myself, Felix, or Taber accompany Robin each day to meet with Daisy."

"Daisy's presence here is my decision, but it does alert us to an obstacle you're going to face. Let's sit." Touching the small of Tabitha's back, he led her to the table and pulled out a chair for her. Felix took the one closer to the door, giving Ty the opposite side of her. Adam and Tex sat on opposite sides of the table.

As Rhett took a seat on the other side of Tex, he asked Ty, "What obstacle?"

"Manetka Resort will be opening soon and you're going to have visitors with all different scents. You've put safeguards in place with security and the computer system, to weed out anyone who might cause problems, but that's not going to eliminate everything. At the very least, you're going to pick up lingering scents from someone who's against us that visitors might have had encountered while traveling. You need to be able to weed through that in order to know immediately whether the person before you is a threat."

"He's right," Tex said. "Unlike Avery, I'm not going to hide while others handle the resort. This is my clan and my resort. I'm going to be at the forefront, just as Ben will be. That's why we're seeking additional guards. You're our most trusted guard and you're going to need to learn to decipher the scents."

"I've got a solution." Ty reached toward the coffee pot in the middle of the table and poured himself a mug. "For most of us, separating the scents is natural. In your case, Rhett, being closed off from the outside world for so long has left you with a weakness. I believe Thaddeus might be able to help you learn this skill quickly. While we haven't had someone who needed help with this particular skill, we've had a couple of the ground guards who needed to boost the ability in order to be able to continue working the perimeter. Thaddeus was able to assist with that."

"If he's available maybe he could help Rhett after we interview the possible guards," Tex suggested. "After that, we'll need to get some rest. I was going to discuss this with you and Tabitha, but I trust everyone here. Rhett's going to pull the guards from the short list for another session with him."

"I figured you'd want to test them yourself." Ty nodded.

"They'll be expecting that as well, but they won't be expecting it in the middle of the night." Tex leaned forward, placing his hands on the long mahogany table. "I came here hoping to find a couple additional Elder Guards. We need resort guards but I can't afford to bring in as many people as it would take to fill the positions to keep the clan safe. So, my hope is that the new guards can help train some of the Texas Tigers. Rhett's been trying but there are only so many hours in the day and he already has enough on his plate. As you know, the duties of an Elder Guard are more demanding than some other positions and the best way to see how they work under a little pressure is to wake them up and put them through challenges."

"Sleep deprived." Felix nodded. "Good idea. Styx has been working them hard but they've been working themselves harder. I've seen many of them in the gym after they've finished their sessions. They work together, helping each other to improve. Even though they know they're competing for a position with you, Korbin, or David, they're willing to help each other to be successful. Whoever you chose will be able to help you train others and that's what you need to be successful."

"We knew the Elders who needed to bring on extra guards would need to continue training others, which is why we started this." Adam grabbed one of the muffins from the tray and tore off a piece.

"Styx, Taber, and Tad went to meet with those who had potential before bringing them here. We had to know they were going to make it through the training and if they were security risks," Ty explained. "This is the last time Styx will be in charge of training. It's becoming too much for him and it's interfering with his duty to protect Bethany. He's Shadow's right hand and separating them is risking Bethany's safety."

"Between protecting Bethany, working with Brooklynn, and these potential guards, it's too much for him," Tabitha added. She slid a lose strand of her hair behind her ear. "His mate, Mira, doesn't complain but I can see it's affecting her as well. A few weeks ago, Carran was on a mission in Pittsburgh. He was there to locate Ambrose, the lion shifter who exposed himself to two police officers. One of those officers was Brooklynn Armstrong, Carran's mate."

"She's the one heading up Shifter Peace Keepers, isn't she?" Tex remembered Ty mentioning it, but there hadn't been much shared about it.

"Yes. Once Styx is confident she's ready, they'll begin recruiting additional shifters. There are a couple here that have already been chosen, so they've been working out with the potential guards for other Alphas."

"Ivy is thrilled to know her proposal is being put into action." Tabitha leaned forward to place her hand on Ty's. "Her mates, Turi and Trey, are already working on the changes for the shifter forum to include a tip database."

"Are you recruiting outside of the clan? If so, why aren't you keeping some of the guards I just watched?" Tex's tiger rose inside of him, coming to brush along his skin with the anxiety flowing through him. There were dangers in their world, especially with the clans that were against Tabitha. With the Shifter Peace Keepers team, it would only be a matter of time before they began to move on the opposing Alphas. While it would save many shifters, just as it had with his clan, it also meant there would be death. He hoped none of the blood spilled would be the people he'd come to care about.

"Once our Elders quarters are complete, Ryan and the construction crew will begin on another building. That's where the Shifter Peace Keepers team will stay, with the exception of Carran and Brooklynn. They have a cabin in close proximity to the location of the future building. We won't be bringing the chosen here until the building is complete, and we're keeping

Shifter Peace Keepers under wraps until then, as well. The last thing we need is our enemies finding out about it now. When they travel to other clans, they'll be representing Queen Tabitha." Ty squeezed his mate's hand, giving her comfort when she shifted slightly. "If they're supporters, it will give them protection. If they're not, it could bring further problems. Because of this, we're recruiting from outside our clan as well. Jinx has a couple who have interest, Korbin has one, but we're also going to try to bring some additional species on."

"Other species? You mean like the Kodiak Bears?" The anxiety increased. Adding other animals could cause a whole different set of issues.

"Tad's going to take on a role with the team, as well as others." Ty was being evasive, but pushing wouldn't bring further answers. "He's been doing more for the clan and Carran wants someone we know and trust with Brooklynn. He was the perfect choice because we know he'll keep her safe and he'll be able to pilot them wherever they need to go. Unofficially, I can say he's going to be her second in command."

"Shifter Peace Keepers will eventually help moderate all species, so adding bears, lions, or other shifters onto the team will eradicate future problems," Tabitha added. "We should introduce you to Brooklynn while you're here. She's learned a lot from your clan and that's going to help her spot similar issues with other clans."

"I look forward to meeting her." He pushed back his chair and started to rise. "If you could excuse me, I need some air."

He didn't wait for anyone to reply before moving toward the door. Out of the corner of his eye, he caught Rhett rising to join him and he shook his head. "Stay, get to know them. I'll only be a moment."

"I think—"

"He'll be fine." Ty cut Rhett off before he could finish. "You have ten minutes before the first interviewee should be here."

Ten minutes didn't seem like enough time to clear his head, but he'd have to make it enough. Strolling from the conference room, he headed to the one place that should be empty, the cafeteria. There, he could get a cup of coffee and look out onto the grounds without bumping into anyone who wanted to talk. He didn't want to appear antisocial, but taking a few minutes to get his thoughts back on track was necessary in order to stay focused on the potential guards.

He wanted to blame his scattered thoughts on being back in Alaska but that wasn't all of it. This had been the first place he felt at home, and this trip was making him realize how much he missed it. More than that, his thoughts kept circling back to *her*.

He'd only caught a glimpse of her out of the corner of his eye before she scurried away, but her scent was alluring and drew his tiger forward. Her long ruby red hair shimmered and when she spun around to leave, it fanned out around her. Who was she? What had she been doing spying on the session? Or had she been spying on him? He didn't believe she was a threat. Otherwise, Ty wouldn't have allowed her in the compound, yet there was something suspicious about her sneaking in after the practice started and hiding in the shadows.

More than anything, her eyes drew him in. The amber hue with a warm gold outline held hints of something mysterious. Their gazes locked briefly before she took off, but it was enough for him to want to know what she was hiding. It was more than his tiger wanting to figure out the puzzle. He was intrigued by her and wanted to know more. He vowed to find out who she was—and why she'd been spying on the session.

Chapter Three

Curled up on the sofa, Carleen held a paperback romance novel in her hands but she wasn't taking in the words on the page. Her gaze slid across the lines but her brain didn't retain what she was reading. Even hours later, her thoughts continued to circle back to the man from the gym. In her mind, she could see him standing before her, his toned body itching for her to touch him, to strip off his clothes and see just how defined those muscles were.

She'd heard rumors of the Texas Tigers and the torture their former Alpha had put them through. Was that why she felt drawn to him? The two of them had suffered similar experiences, and now her tigress was reaching out to him on that level. It would have made sense if she wasn't consistently picturing him naked in her mind.

The front door slammed, startling her enough that she jumped off the sofa and the book went tumbling to the floor. "What the hell?"

"Sorry." Thorn stalked farther into the house, heading straight for the kitchen. "I'm just pissed."

"What happened?" She bent to pick up the book, placing it on the coffee table before joining him in the kitchen. "Didn't things go well today?"

"I fucked up. Damn it!" He grabbed a bottle of beer from the shelf and slammed the refrigerator door shut. "I haven't gone up against Milo yet and he hasn't taken part in many of our sessions. He's too busy guarding the Elders. But guess who I got stuck with today?" He pried open the cap and took a long drink, draining nearly half the bottle in a couple swallows.

"Come on, Thorn, it couldn't have been as bad as you're making it out to be. You've trained hard. I've seen how much work you've put into it. If you're not sleeping, you're doing something to prepare. You've got this." After her reaction to the Alpha, she wasn't sure if she wanted him to have the position, but she tried to be supportive. Thankfully, he was too wrapped up in his own anger to smell her uncertainties.

"I fucked up. The chance is gone." He growled and tossed his bottle in the sink, breaking it, and sending glass shards flying. "I need a run."

Before she could say anything, he was gone, leaving her to clean up the glass. With her thoughts drifting back toward the man she spotted earlier, she grabbed a garbage bag and set to work. Every piece of glass she picked up seemed to bring another question to mind about the Alpha. If only she could remember his name, she could stop referring to him as *the man* or *the Alpha*. Thorn mentioned it in passing before, but now her mind was drawing a blank.

Thorn was normally more controlled. He didn't usually let his temper take over, but tonight he had and now she was cleaning up his mess. Piece by piece, she gathered the glass while forcing herself to think about anything other than the Alpha. She needed to figure out how she was going to convince her brother to focus on another clan.

Maybe Ohio was the place they should try for. The clan was beginning to pick up the pieces and they were opening their own resort soon. More than that, it would be a safe place for Tabitha's supporters who were escaping vindictive Alphas. She might be able to do something to assist them. Texas had been a concern for her. They were established, already a large clan and it was likely she wouldn't fit in easily. Unlike Thorn, who would be there with a purpose, she'd be extra baggage.

Thorn had already made it clear to her that he wouldn't take a position with a guard team unless she could come, too. Guilt tinged the edges of her thoughts. She was holding him back, but the idea of going somewhere totally new with no one by her side was almost too much. If it hadn't been for him, she'd have stayed in Mississippi. She would have supported Tabitha behind Lee's back without ever finding the courage to leave. Thorn taught her to protect herself, but she was no match for Lee or his men. She'd have died and knowing Lee, it wouldn't have been a quick death.

A knock on the door startled her, and she jerked as she reached for a large piece of glass that had fallen under the edge of the counter. "Shit!" She pulled her hand back to discover she'd sliced her palm open. Blood pooled in her cupped hand as she reached for a kitchen towel to wrap around the wound. She wasn't concerned about making a mess, but the sight of her own blood made her stomach churn.

The door flew open, leaving her standing there with her mouth open as blood dripped down her wrist and onto the floor. "What the..." The words died on her tongue as she looked up to find the man from the training arena.

"You're bleeding." Not waiting to be invited in, he pushed the door shut and strolled toward her.

"It's nothing." As he came around the sofa toward the kitchen, she stepped back until she was pressed against the island. She wanted to move, but fear and something else she couldn't put her finger on kept her motionless.

"Who did this?"

"No...no one." She stumbled over her answer as he towered over her. "I...glass..."

"I didn't mean to scare you. I smelled the blood and..." He wrapped his fingers around her wrist to bring her injured hand closer and electricity shot through them. Every part of her tingled until she thought her hair might stand on end. "Well, that explains it."

She tried to pull her hand back, but he held onto her. "I...no...I..."

"What?"

She couldn't answer. She couldn't think straight. Even with the current rushing through every cell in her body, she couldn't believe he was her mate. She should have suspected it before. It was the obvious reason for her fantasies about him but her mind didn't want to comprehend it.

"How about we get you cleaned up?" Keeping his hand on her wrist as if he worried she'd run, he plucked the dish towel out of her other hand and held it to her bleeding palm to absorb some of the blood. "Let's get you over the sink and I'll find a first aid kit."

"I could just shift." As the words left her mouth, she realized what it would mean. She'd have to get naked. Nudity never bothered her before, but the idea of being naked in front of him made her second guess herself.

"Not until we get the glass out." He led her over to the sink before removing his hand from her wrist.

"Glass?" She flexed her fingers, straightening her palm, and burning pain shot up her arm.

"I can see a piece of glass wedged in your hand." He moved the towel aside, keeping it close to soak up the blood. "Try not to move your hand. As I came toward you, the glass caught the light and that's how I know it's there. It can't be too deep—"

If it was anyone else bleeding, she wouldn't have had a problem, but her own blood sent her stomach rolling and left her lightheaded. Thorn would've cracked a joke and made her forget about her injury, keeping her attention on something else while he bandaged her, but he wasn't here.

"Whoa, now." He looped his arm around her waist, keeping her upright. "You okay?"

Forcing her eyelids closed, she nodded. "The sight of my blood makes me lose myself. Can you get it out...or get Thorn?"

"Don't worry, I've got you." He brought her closer to his body and hollered for his guard. "Rhett!"

"Huh?" She hadn't met all the Alaskan Tigers, but she couldn't recall anyone named Rhett. Was he the man who'd been with him observing the guards practice?

"Don't worry, he's with me," he told her, just as the other man opened the door and stuck his head in. "Find me a pair of tweezers."

"I could have—" He cut her off with a shake of his head.

"I'm not leaving you to go get them, and you need to keep your hand still."

"My makeup bag is on the bathroom counter and there's a pair in there." She nodded in the direction of the bathroom as Rhett stepped into the cabin. Without another word, he headed down the short hallway toward the bathroom. "There's a small bottle of alcohol in the bag as well."

"Alcohol?" he asked, lifting her off her feet and sitting her up on the counter.

"Rubbing alcohol, not liquor." The back of her legs cooled as she settled on the countertop, a reprieve from the heat coursing through her. "I don't even know your name."

"Tex, the Alpha of the Texas Tigers, but you already know that part...don't you, Carleen?" Her eyebrow shot up in question, bringing a smile to his face. "I saw you watching us. Curiosity got the best of you. Was it because you wanted to know about me, or because you wanted to see how Thorn would do?"

"Maybe a bit of both." His words hit her and her back stiffened. She'd have pulled away, but she was by the corner of the counter where it formed the L, and he was blocking the only way off. "How did you know my name?"

"Thorn. He won't come to Texas without you, which is why we're here." Rhett explained, strolling back into the kitchen, holding out what Tex needed.

Taking the supplies from his guard, Tex turned back to her. "Before a decision could be made concerning Thorn, I needed to interview you as well."

"A package deal means you both must meet the requirements," Rhett stated, moving back from them.

"Wait outside," Tex ordered. "I'm going to clean her up and she'll need to shift. Then we can speak with her."

Over Tex's shoulder, she watched as Rhett paused, appearing uncertain whether he should argue or not. He stood there for a moment, debating, and as he did she felt Tex's muscles tighten as though waiting for a fight. Between the two men there was a single thread of tension along with a twinge of anger coming from the Alpha, making it clear she was missing something. What was happening between them? Any discord shouldn't be aired for another clan to see, even if they were allies. What situation would Thorn be walking into if he took this position?

The seconds ticked by in silence before Rhett started to move again, but it wasn't until the door clicked shut behind him that Tex met her gaze. "What just happened?" she asked.

"Nothing." He unscrewed the cup for the rubbing alcohol and poured some over the tweezers before taking hold of her hand again. "You might want to look away."

"You're lying." Her breath hissed out from between her lips as he wiped away the blood. "Distract me."

"Hmm…" Without looking up at her, his lips curled into a cocky smile.

"Should I tell you what joyful hours I'm imagining as I make you my mate? Or how tempted I am to fuck you right here on the counter and make you mine? Maybe I should fist a handful of your hair so I can pull you back just enough that your neck is arched out to me in offering, waiting for me to rub my scent all over you. To kiss along your tender skin, starting at your earlobe and working down, inch by inch. All the while my hands slip under your skirt, preparing you for when I slide my——"

"Stop." It came out more breathless than she had meant, but she couldn't take another moment of it. Her body was already hot and flustered as images of his words danced through her mind. Each fantasy grew more erotic than the last.

"Why? Are you saying you haven't thought about those very things?"

"I…um…" She forced herself not to pull away from him. "I've been preoccupied. I mean, with concerns of how Thorn would do."

"Let me remove that anxiety. Thorn did fine. He's made the short list and when I came to talk to you, it was up to you whether he'd stay on the list or not."

"Up to me?"

"Like Rhett said, you needed to be on our side if you were going to come to Texas. You'd have to be willing to commit to me as your Alpha." He glanced up at her. "Doesn't seem like I had anything to worry about, now."

She stared into his deep gray eyes. The way the color seemed to swirl around, reminding her of storm clouds, drew her in. His eyes were beautiful, but they held a hint that he had seen too much. Whatever it was he had survived, it left him jaded. Without thinking, she reached up and pressed her fingers to the side of his face. "Maybe now I understand."

"Understand what?" His voice was low and husky, sending goosebumps along her skin.

"Why Thorn wants to be in Texas." She caressed the curve of his cheek with her fingertips, working her way down to his jaw. "We're the same. Our circumstances were different but we're all broken. We can put ourselves back together, time and time again, but the pieces never go back perfectly. There are always scars. Some of them are hidden and some of them are out for the world to see. Either way, they're there."

"You don't look broken." He set the tweezers aside and placed his hands on the counter on each side of her. "You already know more of my backstory than I know of yours. Why don't you tell me why you're so jaded?"

"I—" Before she could finish, Thorn stormed through the door. *Shit...*

Chapter Four

Standing there surrounded by Carleen's scent relaxed muscles within Tex that he hadn't even realized were tight. As she sat on the kitchen counter with her legs on either side of him, it felt more intimate than it was. Maybe that's how things always were with mates. The reaction she had on him and his beast was enough to allow him to forget about his surroundings for a moment. So when Thorn returned, he was thrown off guard for a moment. It was a good thing Rhett was at the door and had entered a step behind him.

"What the fuck is going on here?" Thorn crossed the small living room and was in the kitchen, coming to them faster than he should have been able to. He was a weaker shifter, but more than that, his bulk should have slowed him down.

Tex spun around, giving Carleen his back, and using his body to block her. She was his sister but Thorn's anger was out of control and his tiger was too close to the edge. There was no telling what he might do.

"Thorn, it's nothing."

"Don't give me that shit! You're bleeding." He came around the counter, his fists balled. "I'm not going to stand here and allow it to happen again. Not again."

"It's not him." She tried to get off the counter, but Tex reached back and held her there. "Let me…before this gets out of hand."

"Go shift. Thorn and I will discuss this." He tipped his head back toward the bedrooms.

"Go, Carleen. You don't need to be here for this." Thorn flexed his shoulders.

"Don't be stupid, Thorn." Rhett stood behind him, waiting for him to make a move. "Think this through. Attacking an Alpha will get you killed."

"Fuck that. I'm taking him with me." Thorn snarled.

"Damn it, Thorn." Carleen jumped off the counter, but Tex moved with her, keeping his body in front of her as a shield. "I cut myself when I was cleaning up the glass. If you want to blame someone for my sliced palm, then place the blame where it belongs—on you. You threw the bottle and left."

"What I walked in on seemed like more than that." He wasn't even looking at her, instead keeping his attention focused on Tex—just how Tex wanted it.

"You know how I am. He stopped by to question me and was kind enough to get the glass out of my palm." She took a deep breath and placed her hand on Tex's back. "It's not like you think. Don't ruin your chances because you're jumping to conclusions. Please..."

"Why don't we sit and talk while Carleen shifts and heals?" Noticing the change in the lingering tension, Tex hoped to gain control before things could get out of the hand. "I think it's safe to say that she's not going to leave until she knows you're not going to do something stupid, so we can either take this down a few notches or let me bind her hand to stop the bleeding."

"Fuck it." Thorn looked past him to his sister. "Go shift. I'll keep my temper in check until you're back. But if you're lying to me, I'll kill him."

"Threatening an Alpha—" Tex glanced at Rhett, cutting him off.

"He's protecting his sister and while normally I'd say it's an uncalled-for threat, knowing their history with Lee, it's understandable. Bear in mind understandable is not the same thing as acceptable. If you commit yourself to me, you should know I won't stand for outbursts like this, especially not from my guards. Voicing your opinion is one thing, but threats against any member of the clan is intolerable, especially an Elder. The last thing we need to do is bring problems into the clan. Once this is settled, you're going to need to prove to me that you can keep your temper in check. Otherwise…" He knew what he had to say and what would have to happen, but the realization of those words hit him full force and he fought the urge to turn back to Carleen. "Otherwise, I'm not going to be able to offer you a spot with the clan."

"Don't dangle an opportunity in front of my face just to get me to look away. I'd give up the chance of having any Elder accept me into their clan if it means keeping Carleen safe."

"Holy Hell, Thorn, can't you ever stop." She slammed her hand onto the countertop and blood seeped from the wound. "I told you this is different. I told you what was happening, and yet you continue to go down the same path. You're going to ruin your chance if you don't shut up." As if feeling the moisture building under her palm she glanced down, the blood draining from her face.

"Here." Tex grabbed the rag, careful to keep the blood stain out of view and wrapped it around her hand. "It's nothing. Don't think about it."

"Go shift and get your damn hand healed," her brother snapped.

Tex's gaze went to her face as he felt her stiffen under his touch. Was she scared of him? Her expression was shielded and even touching her, he wasn't sure what she was thinking. He needed to get her alone, so he could find out not only more about the relationship she had with her brother, but more about her in general. She was to be his mate, and while Thorn was on more questionable ground, he hoped they'd both join him in Texas. In what capacity Thorn would be joining them was still up for debate. While she would be his mate and that would influence some of his decision, it would do nothing to influence Rhett. As their main Elder Guard, Rhett was giving him input on the situation and the guards they brought into the clan.

"Go on, it's fine," he assured her as he brought her other hand over her injured one, to keep the towel secure. "Keep this on there until you shift."

"Thanks." She glanced over his shoulder toward Thorn before looking back at him and mouthed the word "sorry" before scurrying away.

Knowing she was about to get naked and shift into her tigress form made him want to go back and join her. It might be a quick shift, but the opportunity to see her in her beast form brought his tiger closer. Instead, he bent down and began to gather up the remaining glass that still littered the floor.

"What were you doing here?" Thorn stepped back up to the end of the counter but when Rhett moved closer, he stopped.

"If you hadn't considered the fact that I would need to question her before considering you for a position within my clan, you're not as clever as I thought you were." He placed the glass shards in the bag and rose, bringing it to the counter. "You come as a package deal, but I must determine this is what she wants and that she'll be loyal. When I arrived, she was already bleeding. Thinking the worst, I came inside. I startled her and a piece of the glass got stuck in her hand."

"Thinking the worst? What does that mean? You thought I was killing her?"

"No." He continued to clean up the rest of the beer bottle before grabbing paper towels to wipe up the blood on the counter. Even with Thorn's anger, the counter would be clean by the time Carleen rejoined them.

"The compound is safe, but after everything the clan has gone through, Tex and many of us expect the worst," Rhett explained. "He reacted as if she was in danger and went to protect her. You should be thankful for that, especially considering she was cleaning up your mess. What if she had been alone? How long would she have been passed out on the floor from the sight of her own blood before you came back?" Rhett shook his head. "I watched you running around the compound. You should have sensed her blood, but you did nothing."

"I was..." Thorn shook his head, his anger deflating.

"When we arrived, I could sense no one else around but my instinct was to react, so that's what I did." He tossed the last of the bloody paper towels into the bag and turned to Thorn. "It was an accident and she'll be fine, but I didn't know that when I rushed in. We have a tigress that relieves her stress by cutting herself. She's getting the help she needs, but it's been a dangerous road with too many close calls. The scent of Carleen's blood brought that to the forefront of my thoughts and I reacted."

"It's likely that Tex picked up on my emotions." Rhett pulled out the bar stool and sank down onto it. "The tigress is my sister and as my tiger caught hold of the scent of blood, it was a reminder to the last time I smelled it. Images of her curled in a ball on the bathroom floor, her will gone..."

"We almost lost her." Tex's attention was on Rhett, but his words were directed at Thorn. "Carleen's fear of blood and the helplessness to stop it mimicked the scent of our tigress's fear of dying. I won't apologize for barging in here or for helping her, but I will agree the move could be seen as an overreaction."

"If you wouldn't have thrown the beer bottle and then took off, none of this would have happened." Carleen's scent drifted toward Tex before he could see her, but a moment later, she was standing in the short hallway, watching them. "I'm fine now, so can we just drop it?"

"No." Thorn crossed his arms over his chest. "There's more to this then what you're telling me."

"Thorn…" There was a twinge of annoyance in her voice, forcing her to pause and take a deep breath. "It's not like what happened with Lucy, so can you please give this a rest? Let Tex and Rhett do what they came here to do and then we can talk."

"Sir." Rhett held up his watch, letting him know they were running out of time.

"We're going to have to continue this later. I have another meeting." He glanced at Thorn and then back to her. "Carleen, I'd like you to join me for dinner. It will give us a chance to have our chat."

"I'd like that." She kept her attention on him, refusing to look at her brother, as if she expected him to be angry. "What time?"

"Give me an hour and I'll come for you." He tipped his head to Rhett, motioning for him to head toward the door, and came around the counter to stand in front of her. "You'll be okay now?" He kept his voice low, hoping she understood the double meaning in his question, without alerting Thorn.

"Fine." She brushed her hand along his forearm, careful to keep the touch hidden from her brother. She clearly didn't want to upset him, but she couldn't stop herself from touching Tex one last time. "I'll see you then."

After seeing the fear in her eyes earlier, he didn't like leaving her alone, but there wasn't much he could do right then. He had to meet with Ty, while Rhett needed to dig into their background further. Something wasn't in the file that Ty had given them, and he needed to know what it was before any decisions could be made. If they were a danger to his clan, he couldn't take them back to Texas, no matter the personal cost to him.

Standing next to her dresser as she prepared for dinner with Tex, Carleen could feel the silence hanging over her. Silence was something she normally treasured. In Mississippi, there never seemed to be enough of those quiet alone moments. Now she cursed it. She wanted Tex to return, giving her something else to focus on. She was tired of thinking about the situation with her brother.

The tension between her and Thorn had never been as bad as it had been the last several weeks. Until he arrived to find Tex between her legs while she sat on the counter, she wasn't sure things could get worse between them. Now she realized they could. Convincing him that he was reading the situation wrong was impossible. He was angry, mostly with himself for messing up during the training session earlier, and now she was the one who had to deal with it. Thorn always had his moody times, but it wasn't until the mess with Lucy that things became unbearable and he began to take his moods out on those around him, particularly her.

He was her best friend, the one person who would always have her back. Lately the relationship seemed one-sided. She was there for him, but when she needed his support, he had nothing for her. Thorn was the last person she could confide in when it came to the situation with Tex. She wasn't sure how he would react, but if he got a position with the Texas Tigers, he'd never feel as though he'd done it himself. In his mind, it would always be his connection to her that secured him the position. It wouldn't matter what the truth was, or that he was good enough to make the team without her influence.

"Damn you, Thorn." Sliding the tube of lip gloss over her lips as she stood before the mirror, she cursed him for throwing the beer bottle. If she hadn't been cleaning up after him, she wouldn't have cut herself. Maybe one slight change in their brief encounter would have been enough to hold off discovering they were mates for just a bit longer, allowing Thorn to be chosen for one of the positions on his own.

She tugged her hair from the ponytail she'd pulled it into earlier and let the strands fall around her shoulders. The deep red color looked like spun rubies and had always been one of her favorite features about herself. The way it shined brought out her eyes, though lately all it seemed to do was bring attention to her pale skin, making her look worse than before. Running her hands through her hair, she tried to fluff it the best she could.

Since Thorn left for the celebration with the other guards who had auditioned, she had spent the time changing from one outfit to another, trying to find something perfect. On some level, her tigress wanted to impress Tex because he was her mate, yet she barely even knew him. Would their mating be like her parents, unhappy and bitter, or would it be something special like she always dreamed it would be?

With the kindness in his touch and the way he took care of her wound, she wanted to believe it would be different than what she had witnessed her whole life. Still, she couldn't get her hopes up. She needed to be prepared for whatever the future held. More than that, she'd have to put on a show just as her mother had all those years. If the mating with Tex became an unhappy union, she wouldn't just have to convince Thorn that things were fine, but the whole clan. They had to believe she was happy or not only her life, but also Tex's would be in danger. *Am I up for that task?*

A light rap on the front door forced her to stop messing with her hair and take one final look in the mirror. Staring at her reflection, she second-guessed her decision to wear the black slacks and emerald green sweater. Maybe she should have kept it relaxed with jeans. Did she appear as if she was trying too hard?

As the knocking grew louder, she forced herself to forget about her appearance and go to the door. This connection between them wasn't based on looks or even personality. He was an attractive man and she found herself drawn to him in the gym. Maybe on some level, her tigress already recognized him and it was pushing them together. She wasn't sure, but she had to remember that what was happening was based on their beasts, nothing more.

In the living room, she took a deep breath and tried to calm herself. She needed to stay friendly and keep an open mind. Worrying she'd end up in an unhappy mating would do nothing to stop the inevitable; it would just cause her undue stress. She pulled open the door to find Tex standing on the porch looking better than he did an hour ago. Like her, he had also changed. He was still in jeans but his t-shirt had been replaced with a V-neck sweater, allowing her the briefest glimpse of his toned chest. The tanned skin of his chest and the curves of his muscles under the sweater made her want to see more of him naked.

"Ready?"

"Yeah, sure. Where are we going?" She glanced past him, expecting to see Rhett, but no one was around.

"My cabin." He pointed a few buildings over. "It will give us more privacy, and I managed to snag dinner from the ladies."

"Which ladies?" She stepped onto the porch and pulled the door shut behind her. "You know, I could have cooked."

"Kallie's mates, Taber and Thorben, smoked the fresh salmon they caught this morning. While Milo, Jayden, and Drew manned the grill with steaks and burgers. Kallie, Robin, Harmony, and some of the other clan females brought a ton of different side dishes. Tabitha assured me there was a little of everything waiting for us at the cabin." He led the way toward his cabin.

"You should be there." Sidestepping to avoid a slick pile of snow, her shoulder brushed along his, sending currents tingling through her.

He reached out to take hold of her arm under the pretense of making sure she was steady on her feet, but from the way his gray eyes sparkled, it was clear there was more to the touch. Had he wanted to touch her ever since she opened the door?

"I'd rather be with you, but if you'd like to go…"

"No." Her answer was too quick, causing his eyebrows to arch together as his gaze narrowed down on her. "I mean…Thorn said you were only here for a couple days. Don't you want to spend time with your friends?"

"There will be other times." With his hand on the small of her back, he led her inside his temporary living quarters. "I expected Thorn to still be pissed off when I returned."

"He's out with the other guards, having a celebration. With all the time they've spent together, they've grown close and after tomorrow, they'll be separated. For them, tonight is about letting off some steam. Plus, to be honest, I needed the break from him as much as he needed to go out with the guys. He's in such a…" She let her words trail off as they stepped inside. She felt comfortable enough around him to discuss the situation, but talking about Thorn like that might cost him an opportunity. She couldn't risk it.

"Thorn's temperament is not lost on me, so there's no reason to censor yourself." He closed the door and turned back to her. "Are you afraid of him?"

"What? No." She stared at him in disbelief. "Why would you say that?"

"Your eyes." His hand slipped over hers, interlocking their fingers so his palm was against the back of her hand. "When you looked at Thorn earlier, there was fear in your eyes. I wanted to pull you aside and find out why."

"I wondered why you were asking me if I'd be fine. I knew you didn't mean about the blood since I was healed, but I wasn't sure why you were concerned." She closed her hand, cupping his fingers to her palm. "Thorn would never hurt me. He's my best friend and my protector. He's become a little more protective lately, but after what happened with Lucy, I understand."

"I'm going to need to know what happened. The whole story, not the two short notes that are in his file." He brought his free hand up to her face and let his index finger trail down the curve of her jaw before bringing it to her lips. "You smell like peaches."

"Peaches, huh? Do you like peaches?"

"My favorite when they're fresh, but even then, they have nothing on you." He ran his finger over her lips, teasing lightly along the bottom before going over the top. "Do you know how bad I want to fucking kiss you?"

The heat of his breath tingled along her skin, enticing her tigress. "Go ahead." She wasn't sure if it was the moment, or her beast urging her forward, but she was ready to go with the flow because she wanted it, too.

He guided her backward until her back was pressed against the wall and his chest brushed against hers. Leaning his head down toward her, she thought he was going to do it. Excitement and nervousness rushed through her, heightening her senses. His lips hovered over hers and she debated closing the distance.

"Tempting."

"Huh?" She wasn't sure what he meant by that. He acted like he was going to kiss her, so why didn't he?

"You." He leaned back just enough that he wasn't pressed against her. "You're tempting, but we need to talk first. Otherwise, we'll never get to that part."

"You just want my story so you can figure out what to do about Thorn. Otherwise you wouldn't have stopped." She pulled her hand from his and slipped out from between him and the wall. Moments ago, she wanted to put distance between them, to get her thoughts together and stop the mating desire from influencing her. Now that they were no longer touching, she missed it. The inner struggle between her human side and her beast never seemed as strong as it did at that moment.

Her beast wanted to jump his bones while the human side of her wanted to know the man she was about to sleep with. The alternative to denying a mate was going rogue. To most, that was a choice worse than death. To her, it might be a lesser evil. She needed to know him before she committed her body and soul to him. Yet, when he was near, those thoughts disappeared and her tigress gained control. It had only been a few hours since they discovered they were mates and already she was losing the battle against her beast's natural instincts. How bad would it get before she had no choice but to give in to him?

"Sure, I need to know about Lucy and Thorn's moodiness, but I really want to know you. Just as I'm sure there are things you want to know about me." He strolled past her and headed toward the kitchen. "Let's eat. We don't have to rush this."

Rush? Was that what they were doing? It felt natural, but she was taken aback by his words. Maybe her tigress was taking more control when it came to the connection between them. Even though she had promised to fight it until she knew more about him, she was failing. Even knowing that, she was disappointed it had ended so quickly. She wanted to feel his lips on hers, even if it was only a light touch. Soon…

Chapter Five

The tension in the air between them made dinner an uneasy event. Tex had tried to make small talk but he found himself drifting into his own thoughts. The scent of her next to him, yet out of reach, made him want to pull her close. Temptation to touch her was there but he denied himself that pleasure. She was hiding something and he needed to know what it was before they could move forward. Mating might solidify things between them, giving him a clear insight, but he would prefer to learn more from her directly—to discover the truth before they went down the road of no return.

"I guess the time has come." She dried the last dish and set it in the counter before turning back to him. "Where do you want me to start?"

"I've been trying to think of a way to put you at ease and slowly work the conversation to it, but there's no easy way." He set his beer bottle aside and came to stand in front of her. "Every time Lucy's name is mentioned, your muscles go stiff and you shut down, blocking me out."

"No, I don't."

"Really?" He brought his hands up to her shoulders, gently rubbing small circles along her tight muscles. "Relax. Nothing you tell me is going to have me running out the door. We can face whatever it is together."

Together. That sounded better than he expected it to. All his life, he had been alone and now he had a mate to spend the rest of his days with. It was a change and would take time to adjust to. Still, there was something exciting about it, too. He just wasn't sure if she felt the same way. What did she think of this whole mating business? There were times she seemed open to it while the next second, she closed him out.

"Just because you don't run, doesn't mean you're actually here. Someone can be physically present without being there mentally or emotionally."

"I'm here for you, Carleen, always and in every way." He stopped rubbing her shoulders and drew her close. Hugging her to him, he ran his hands down her back. The way she spoke of someone mentally checking out made him wonder if he was wrong about Lucy being dead. Maybe she wasn't physically dead, but rather a shell of her former self. "This secret is tearing you apart and there's no reason to carry this burden by yourself."

"It's a weight Thorn carries, too. He blames himself. It was his job to protect her and he failed, but he doesn't know I'm just as responsible." She let out a sigh and leaned against his chest. "Lucy…we left her…"

"Who's Lucy?"

"My sister…our sister…Lee's mate." Her body shook with unshed tears.

"Shit!" He squeezed her tighter to him. "Carleen—"

"I knew it would change things. Thorn knew it would cost us a place in another clan. He wanted to forget, pretend Lucy wasn't our sister, but I can't and now I cost Thorn his chance." She pulled back from him but with the counter behind her, there was nowhere for her to go.

"Bullshit." He dropped his arms away from her but didn't move, instead leaning back enough to look down at her. "This didn't cost you or him anything, nor did it change things."

"But—"

"Listen for a minute." The urge to hold her again was there but he kept his arms at his side, giving her space. "Lee's the Alpha of the Mississippi Tigers and while we don't believe he's as bad as some other Alphas, he's still an issue. One that we'll have to deal with in the future, which puts your sister at risk. My comment wasn't out of anger, just concern for Lucy."

"Thorn says she's already dead, that she's not our sister anymore." Tears swam in her eyes. "She's not the same but she's still my sister. I knew what he was like and I still..."

"Still what?" He pressed her when she fell silent.

"Encouraged her to embrace her mate." She slipped past him and walked toward the window in the living room. "My parents' mating was anything but happy. There was no romance or love. They hated each other. To him, Mom was too weak and Dad acted like an asshole more often than not, making it clear he hated being stuck in the mating. They could barely say two civil words to each other. Every time one of them spoke, it always ended up in a fight. They accepted the mating because it was better than the alternative."

He made his way into the living room and came to stand a few feet behind her. She appeared to be staring out the window, yet he didn't believe she was seeing anything out there. Her vision was filled with memories of her parents. How did this tie in with Lucy and Lee? He wasn't sure, but he'd let her tell the story at her own pace.

"I had just turned eighteen and while I was terrified I'd end up with a mating like my parents, I wanted it over. I wanted to find him so I knew what I had to deal with. The suspense of it was killing me. I wanted a mating filled with love and romance or at the very least, one in which we could stand each other without abuse. When Lucy found out she was to be Lee's mate, I started to lose hope I could even have that. She was the oldest, and being mated to Lee meant she would follow in our parents' footsteps."

She turned to him. "Then he started courting her. He was a different man. He was sweet, brought her flowers, had a special dinner for her. The change wasn't just with her, but everyone. She voiced concerns about the age

45

difference. Lee was thirty-one and Lucy was nineteen. Mom brushed them off, telling her not to worry. With our lifespan, it's not the same as it is for humans. A few days later, when Lucy and I were alone, she told me that wasn't her only fear. The night before, Lee had grabbed her hard enough to leave bruises and she was terrified the change wouldn't last. She didn't want to be at his mercy and she was willing to take…"

"Suicide?" He was able to keep his voice flat but he was still surprised. Mating brought their beasts closer to the surface and the longer things continued without completing the mating, the worse things would become. It sounded like Lucy and Lee had discovered they were mates after only a couple of days. She must've had enough control over her beast in the beginning in order to consider the alternative, showing how terrified she was of the prospect of mating with Lee.

"She was always very vocal about the fact that she didn't want to live with a mate like our father. I was envious of her devotion to her beliefs because I didn't think I was strong enough to take my own life. A life of misery had to be better than no life." She took a sidestep and dropped down onto the recliner near the window. "I talked her out of it. I wanted to believe Lee had changed. More than that, I was selfish. I didn't want to lose my sister, my best friend."

"It's not your fault." He crouched in front of the chair and took her hands in his. "If she truly wanted to, you couldn't have stopped her."

"The next day he forced her to complete the mating and she was gone. No more late night talks, no more morning runs. Everything changed. I guess I hadn't expected that, but for a while things were okay. Slowly he started cutting her off from us, breaking her will more every day. Now she's just a shell of her former self. She's there physically, but other than that, my sister is gone."

"How long have they been mated?" His chest tightened as he waited for her answer. Was it too late to save her?

"Four years." The answer came out on little more than a whisper. If he hadn't been a shifter, he wouldn't have even heard it.

"Fuck!" Too much time had passed to ensure Lucy could survive the death of her mate, especially if her will was indeed broken. "Does Ty know?"

"No!" Her body jerked and she stared into his eyes. "No...don't...we can't."

"Come here." He crossed the room and pulled her to her feet, then sat in a chair and tugged her down onto his lap. "I can't allow him to authorize a team to go to Mississippi without this information. He wanted to go after Lee because of the issues in Connecticut, but he didn't because you and Thorn had just arrived. Lee's guard would have been up and the death toll would have increased. Instead, Ty used this time to try to convince Lee committing to Tabitha was the right thing to do, but he's unwilling. You understand Tabitha's rule has to be complete for the future to change."

"Connecticut? What issue?"

"Heidi's brother, Harry, came for her after her mate died. She committed herself to David and the clan, but Harry wasn't willing to accept that. He attempted to attack Victoria. Before he could, David stepped in. Harry was killed in order to protect Victoria and the clan." He ran his hand down her back, trying to keep her calm. "Harry's visit proved one thing—the Mississippi Tigers are a threat. They're against Tabitha and everything she stands for. You know that already."

"Not everyone."

"You're right, but those in charge are and that makes them a threat. Not just to Tabitha and the future she's trying to create but to everyone who supports the change. Lee's already made his intentions clear. He's not going to stand by while his kind commits to her and he'll do whatever he can to destroy those who support her." Needing more contact, he slipped his hand under the back of her sweater. There was nothing sexual about it; he did it to comfort his beast. Skin to skin contact would ease the anxiety rising within him, but would also help push back the tension within her.

"I knew there would be a war before we had peace but I hadn't considered the cost." She tucked her hair behind her ear and sighed. "I knew many would die but what I didn't know was how high the personal price would be. A selfish part of me wonders if it's worth it. Then I look at you and I know it is."

Not knowing what to say to that, he remained silent. He had those same moments where he questioned everything they were doing. In the end, there was no other alternative. They had to push forward and make a safer world for themselves. They could no longer allow Alphas like Avery to remain in command and abuse clan members.

"When is the cost too great to justify the cause? Lucy…Thorn…you. It's too much."

"I know." He tipped his head to press his lips to the top of her head. "I wish I could tell you everything will be fine—"

"You can't. I know as well as you do that Lucy is going to die. She might be the first, but she won't be the last. How long before I lose you and Thorn?" Her body shook and silent tears rolled down her face. "I don't know if I can take it."

"You're stronger than you give yourself credit for." He reached up and wiped the tears from her cheeks. "I'll do everything I can to keep you and those you care about safe."

"By putting yourself in more danger." She pulled out of his embrace and rose from his lap. "That's just it, I don't want to lose you either. The tightness in my chest at the very thought scares me because I don't know you. The fear of losing you is all because of this mating desire and my tigress. What if we can't stand each other? How can I dread losing you when I don't even know if I can live with you?"

"Mates are compatible on every level. We complete each other."

"You've never been around two mates who hate each other, have you?" She stood in front of him, watching him closely for a moment. Before he had a chance to reply, she added, "My parents hated each other with every fiber of their beings. Anger was like a beating pulse in our house. If it's the same for us, I shouldn't care if you're killed helping Tabitha and Ty. Yet, I do."

"It's not going to be the same for us." He forced himself to stay in the chair instead of going to her like he wanted to. She needed space and he'd respect that. "I've seen enough torture and hatred in my past. I refuse to have my future filled with it. We're going to have the happiness we both want and deserve."

"You can't be sure of that."

"Really?" He rose and before she could step farther away from him, he wrapped his arms around her waist and pulled her tight against him. "Our beasts bring our mates to us and they're responsible for the sexual desire, but the rest is just us."

"What do you mean?" Her voice was low and seductive, making him want to do so much more than just hold her.

"The desire to protect you is all me."

"You're an Alpha. You want to protect those under you. Once again, it's natural." She tried to reason, but he shook his head.

"You're not mine, meaning not part of my clan…at least not yet. This impulse to protect you shouldn't be there but it is, because you're mine. You're my mate, not because my tiger demands it. There's something between us, something that urges me on. When I touch you…" He slipped his fingers under the back of her sweater, teasing along the top of her slacks. "You have to feel that."

"It's the mating desire. It has to be. It couldn't be anything else. You don't know me."

"It's more than that. As Alpha of my clan, I feel the connections with my members. The mating desire is different."

"You can feel their mating desires?" Her brows knitted together in confusion. "I thought it was shared only between those mated."

"A strong Alpha with control over his clan will feel it. It's not the same as what they're going through, but there're pieces that come through the connection. I can feel if they let it go for so long that their beasts are rising, and it's my duty to step in to make sure that doesn't happen." His lips curled into a smile before he chuckled. "The first time, it was shocking, but it's incredible to see them to come together. It reminded me why I'm committed to what we're doing and it reaffirmed that I did the right thing when I agreed to take over the clan."

"How did you come to take over? I mean, I've heard rumors. Lee didn't like talk of other clans, so I never knew the truth. Did you really go back by yourself to kill Avery and save your clan?"

"No." Her question brought up images of Avery's final moments, pulling him away from reality. The next moments would send him spiraling back to the past, and he knew he should step away from her but he couldn't. Their touch would pull her down with him but as the darkness filled his vision, he frozen in place, unable to do anything. Physically he was still in Alaska, standing in one of the guest cabins with his hands around Carleen, but he couldn't see any of that. His vision filled with darkness and even without the chill in the air or the musty, blood filled scent that lingered, he knew he'd returned to the tunnels. They'd since been filled in and closed up, so they no longer ran under Manetka Resort, but they remained alive in his memories.

"Get the hell out of the way or I'll shoot you. I won't stand here while he hurts anyone." Jinx's words brought Tex to his side.

"Summer is his sister," he explained to Jinx before looking at Ben. "We'll save her if you get out of the way. Come with us and get her out of there yourself." He wanted Ben to make the decision himself, to choose to fight back and save his sister and everyone else from the horrors occurring so close by. Before Ben could make the decision, Styx reached forward, snatched the boy's gun away from him, and pushed him aside.

"We don't have time for your games."

"Cover me." Jinx pulled the door open, and a flood of screams poured out. A woman lay stretched out on the table, blood everywhere. "Step away from the woman!"

"What the fuck!" Avery glanced to the door, an instrument resembling a scalpel in his hand. "How did you get in here?"

"Tex…" Through the haze of his memory, he could hear Carleen calling to him but the memory wouldn't let him go.

"Through the door." He stood next to Jinx, and the others who had come with him flanked them. He knew some of them had their doubts about his presence, but as Avery's jaw dropped, he knew he had done the right thing. He needed to be there, and he needed Avery to know who had led them there. "Years ago, before you beat the will out of me, I told you someday someone would stop you. Well, that day has come and I'm one of the people who plan to stop you."

"Boy, you don't stand a chance." Avery's laughter sliced through the stillness in the air and clawed at Tex, making him angrier.

"Not alone, but as a whole we do."

"Where did you find them? They must be a bunch of solitary shifters, because no Alpha would dare take me on." The cockiness was clear in Avery's tone as it was anytime

someone made the slightest move against him.

"I don't believe we've had the pleasure of meeting. I'm Jinx, the West Virginia Alpha, and this is Ty, Alpha of the Alaskan Tigers." Jinx tipped his head to Ty, standing on the other side of him. "One Alpha might not, but Ty and I are nothing like the others. We'll fight for what's right, no matter the cost. Now, I told you once to step away from the woman."

"What do you think this will accomplish?" Avery lowered the scalpel before shoving it into the woman's chest.

"Fuck." Tex trained his gun on Avery, ready to shoot, but he was too late. Jinx had already squeezed the trigger, the first of many shots that rang out.

Chapter Six

Pulled into the darkness with Tex, Carleen was left with no choice but to hold on. Fighting wouldn't help things and he was no use as he mumbled to himself. Standing in the cold, damp tunnel made her uneasy, while the strong scent of fear permeating the air brought her tigress forward. Logically she knew there was nothing there that could hurt her. This flashback was a ghost from his past and neither of them were there now. As the door in front of them opened and the horrid scent of blood filled her lungs, she clung to that knowledge.

Tex stood in front of her, gun at the ready as he moved through the door to join another man, someone she didn't recognize. "I'm one of the people who plan to stop you." The rest of the men moved closer, showing their support as Tex faced off with the other man. Instantly, she understood who was standing before them—Avery.

"Tex…" She tried to call to him, to bring them out of this flashback, but he didn't flinch.

Helpless to stop the situation, she stayed near him, watching her mate relive the final moments of Avery's life. Refusing to look at the bleeding woman on the table, she kept her attention on Tex. His body was stiff but ready for whatever might happen. The darkness in his eyes made her wonder if he had been willing to die that day if it meant freeing the Texas Tigers from Avery's control.

Was he locked in the memories of the past because of her? When she'd asked about him becoming Alpha, had it brought this on? How much of his past lingered just under the surface, waiting for openings to seep through into the present?

Watching him raise the gun, she was brought back to what was happening and she reached out to him. Not there in the flashback, but where their actual bodies were back in the cabin. She could feel her fingers caress his face and his body tremble under her touch. His beast was so close to the surface that she could feel the fur brush along her body. "Tex…come on, Tex. Come back to me."

"You're fucking dead."

The harshness of his tone brought her out of the flashback and back to the cabin. Not wanting to startle him, she stayed absolutely still in his embrace. Even her voice refused to work, though she wasn't sure what she'd say to him. His body was tense and his eyes were closed, making her wonder if he was still trapped in his flashback alone. She almost wished she could go back, not so she could see what happened but so she could be there for him.

His eyelids sprang open, revealing a fiery orange glow, and for a moment, she swore he was going to shift but just like that it was gone. His normal stormy gray irises returned, full of pain and sorrow, making her hold him tighter. "Tex?"

"Fuck!" His arms dropped from her waist but before he could step away, she grabbed hold of his shirt.

"Don't push me away." With one hand on his cheek and the other holding tight to his shirt, she willed him to stay.

"I could have hurt you."

"Never." Hoping he wouldn't pull away from her, she cupped his face between both hands. "You weren't here but you were. Your beast knows my scent. Even if you don't believe you had enough control, he did. Your tiger would never hurt me, and neither would you."

"You weren't so sure of that a few minutes ago."

"I know it now." She lifted her hand to grab hold of his white cowboy hat and pull it off. "Oh, Tex…"

"Don't!" he snapped, stilling her mid-motion.

"What?" Her voice squeaked and she almost dropped his hat back on his head.

"Don't look at me like that. I don't want your sympathy."

"Sympathy…baby, you couldn't be more wrong." She dropped the cowboy hat on the chair they'd vacated minutes before and turned back to him. "You're my fucking hero."

"That's worse. I'm no one's—"

"Don't." She pressed her finger to his lips. "You saved them. While it doesn't erase the memories or the scars, and it doesn't bring back those he murdered, you put an end to his destruction. That means everything."

"We arrived too late." The sorrow was clear in his voice and in his eyes.

Since she witnessed his flashback, there was no doubt in her mind he meant they had been too late to save the woman Avery had been torturing. "Who was she?"

"Who?" His eyebrows knitted together in confusion.

"The woman Avery was killing when you arrived. I could see her—"

"You what?" He pulled away from her before she could stop him and paced the small space in front of the sofa. With every click of his cowboy boots, the tension in the air seemed to be emphasized, making her uneasy.

"Your flashback…I don't know how, but I was there. I saw her. Even parts I didn't see, I know what happened. It's not possible, but I have knowledge of events I shouldn't. I don't understand it." She held her breath, watching him, waiting for his reaction. "I realize you're upset and I'm sorry, I really am, but it's not my fault."

"No, it's mine." He growled. "I should go."

"Go?" She stepped into his path, blocking his exit. "Just like that, you're going to leave? You're not going to explain anything. You're just going to walk out on me."

"What do you want me to do?"

"How about you explain what the hell just happened?" She wanted to reach out and touch him. Instead, she crossed her arms over her chest. "Don't throw a wall up between us now. You've been pushing me to accept what's happening between us, but with the first sign of troubled waters, you're ready to run." Realization dawned on her, causing her chest to vibrate as her lips curled up in a smile, and suddenly she was chuckling. It was out of place, but it felt right.

"What the fuck is so funny?"

"Where were you going to go?" She shook her head, unable to believe she was laughing at something so ridiculous. Surely, he could find somewhere to hide out until she gave up waiting on him or he was ready to face her, but it didn't seem like him. "This is your cabin. You're not in Texas, where I'm sure there're plenty of places you could escape to. You're in Alaska. Are you going to go to Ty and tell him your mate is in your cabin, refusing to leave, and you need somewhere else to stay? I can't see my scary Alpha telling others he's having trouble with his woman."

"Your scary Alpha?" His gaze centered in on her.

"I...um..." She fought not to take a step back as he crept closer.

"Is that what I am?"

In a blink of an eye, he closed the distance between them and pressed her against the half wall dividing the living room from the entryway. He lifted her up to sit on the ledge of the wall and without second guessing herself, she wrapped her legs around his waist, keeping him close. "Tex…"

"Answer me." He leaned in closer and took a deep breath. "Peaches?"

"Yes…" With her hands pressed against his chest, she was torn between pushing him back so she could see his face, and allowing her hands to roam over the tightness she felt hidden under his sweater. A growl vibrated his chest, but there was nothing threatening to it; the noise seemed more comforting than anything, and she allowed her fingers to caress downward. "Kiss me."

"After what you saw—"

"Don't." She let her eyelids drift shut and allowed her beast to push her in the right direction. Her tigress would know what she needed to say, without allowing her human side to overthink things. "Earlier in the kitchen I was terrified of you, while drawn to you at the same time. It was unnerving, but what I saw allowed me to understand you better. You're different than I originally thought."

"How's that?" His breath caressed her face.

"Since Thorn forced me to leave Mississippi, I've been terrified Lee would find us. More than that, I've been terrified of who our next Alpha will be. Thorn told me I was worrying for nothing, that anyone would be better than Lee, but I wasn't convinced. I heard rumors of what happened in Texas and an Alpha like that wouldn't be any better, it would be worse. Lee's strict, and discipline is just a form of torture for him, but he doesn't do it out of sport like Avery did." She opened her eyes and looked into his. "I only caught a glimpse of what happened there, but you give me hope. You not only survived but you went back and saved your people. Do you realize how many people would be too afraid of even going back, let alone taking on the task of rebuilding the clan?"

"I didn't do it to prove anything."

She knew he hadn't, but that didn't change the outcome. Every stride he took was proving a clan could be saved with a strong Alpha in command. While some had been lost along the way, the majority of the members had been saved and they were stronger than ever before. He might not want to recognize it, but it was happening and he was responsible for it. It gave her hope that maybe the members of the Mississippi Tigers could be saved, if they could take Lee out of power.

Lucy will— She cut herself off, refusing to go down that road. Instead, she focused on the man before her and as she did, she realized how he ended up taking over the clan.

"You did it because Ben suggested you take over the clan. He believed you could lead them out of the darkness and into the light." She leaned back from him so she could get a better look at him. "How do I know that? I can practically see you standing at the podium in front of your clan. The guys from your flashback are there with you. Ben and some woman are there, too. How do I even know who Ben is?" Panicking, her heart sped and her beast rose as it searched for the invisible threat.

"Peaches, it's okay." He pulled her back against him. "Everything is okay."

"How can you say that?" Nothing was okay about this situation. Something strange was going on. She had never seen something so clearly about another person like she had with him. She never heard of the mating connection doing this before. "What's happening to me?"

"Shh, sweetie. Everything is going to be fine. I told you before this was my fault and it is." He rubbed circles along her back but was no longer looking at her. "I was a guard for Avery, but I never actually guarded him. Unlike others, I never had to keep my emotions in check constantly. Since I found out you're my mate, I haven't been shielding from you. It wasn't something I decided to do. My shields just slipped. Some of that might have been to put you at ease, while part of it could've been wanting someone to understand me completely. The parts of me that I can share with my mate are parts I can't share with anyone else. It could be taken as a weakness, and while the clan has come a long way, it would still make me vulnerable."

"I don't understand. Elders have to shield constantly or their emotions affect their clan. You can't drop them for one person and keep the shields up from others."

"With practice, you can." He dropped his gaze back down to her. "When Adam was in Texas searching for Robin, his mate who was being hunted down by Pierce's gang, he ran into some issues and I was sent to secure the helicopter so that he could make a quick escape. It didn't go as planned, but now I realize that was the best fuckup of my life."

"What do you mean? What happened?" she pressed.

"Before Adam and Robin could board the helicopter and get out of town, Pierce's men attacked us. I was shot, and knowing Avery would have seen my injuries as a failure, I refused to shift to heal myself. I wanted to give in to my injuries and let death claim me. Instead, Adam brought me to Alaska, to their healer." His eyes closed, as if remembering what happened, but thankfully, he didn't pull them both back into a flashback. "I was angry at first because being alive meant I would have to face Avery. He'd be angrier since I didn't return straight away. His rage would mean unbelievable pain. It was Robin who got through to me and showed me that I didn't have to return to Texas, that I could stay in Alaska if I wanted to." His sadness thickened the air until it was overwhelming

"You returned and took Avery down." She tugged his sweater up so that her hands were touching his bare stomach. Unlike before, when she wanted to explore the contours of his chest, all she wanted to do now was offer whatever comfort she could.

"Knowing I had somewhere else to stay, I focused on healing myself mentally, emotionally, and physically. I used my time to build strength, extend my weapons knowledge, and most of all get into the mental space I needed in order to deal with Avery. Robin was a tremendous help during all of this, especially when it came to moving past what happened. She was going to college for her master's degree in psychology and by the time she found us, she only had one semester left. Since then, she's finished her degree and is working with shifters. It's something we've needed for a long time and I can attest to the good she's doing. Her help was essential in bringing the clan together."

As he spoke of Robin, his lips curled into a smile. She was special to him—as a friend, nothing more. The connection he had with Robin was enough for Carleen to know she had pegged the woman correctly when they'd first been introduced. "I met her."

"I figured. Her mate is part of the Elder team and has worked with the potential guards, so it's likely she'd have been around."

"No, I mean I met her before we came here." She pulled her hands out of his sweater and dropped them to her lap. "When we left Mississippi, there was no plan. Late one night after everyone fell asleep, Thorn sneaks into my bedroom and tells me to throw a few things into a bag, that we're leaving. I had five minutes and we were gone. Next thing I know we're in the middle of nowhere, Colorado, hiding out in an old, abandoned farmhouse. Thorn knew about the online shifter forum and he reached out to the bears who run it to see if they could help us find a safe clan. The next day Styx, Adam, and Robin showed up. I was terrified. I didn't know who they were or how they found us. Robin pulled me aside while the guys talked."

"She has a way of making you see there's still brightness in the world even though you're feeling utterly helpless."

Not knowing what else to say, she nodded. Robin's words got her to see that they couldn't stay at the abandoned farmhouse. They had to move on and commit themselves to an Alpha and a clan if they wanted to survive. Until they did, Lee would hunt them down.

"We're straying from my point again. What I was trying to tell you is that while I was here in Alaska, I changed. So, when I returned I was in a different mindset than the rest of the clan. Their terror was crushing. It was like a tidal wave before I stepped into the position of Alpha. After I did, everyone's emotions became overwhelming."

"Their fear of the future was suffocating you. Shortly after we arrived, Ty told me I had to gain control over my worries because they were making the air heavy. It can be hard to breathe when it's like that."

"Exactly," he agreed. "Ty helped me gain control of it. He taught me how to connect with the clan without suffering through every emotion with them. At first, I wanted to shut down. He made me realize that by blocking them, I was hurting the clan. Dividing them from me would have left us vulnerable and I couldn't have that. With my new position, I also had to shield them from me. I couldn't let them feel my fear or doubt, or they'd have it, too. They needed someone strong to lead them. Once I had that under control, he taught me how to drop my shield for just those I needed to. Allowing Ben or our guards to know what was happening. That was critical."

"I thought that came naturally for Elders. One of the last conversations I had with Lucy, she told me I needed to keep my emotions in check or she wouldn't be able to hold Lee back. She could feel how distraught I was over losing the close bond I had with her. Trust me, Lee wouldn't have taught her shit, so it had to come naturally."

"Most Alphas have fought for their position. I might have been working toward an Elder position one day, but the last time he saw me..." Tex paused and shook his head.

"What?" she pressed.

"Let's just say I was a weak shifter before my time here. Avery made sure we all were. Here, everything changed. Each of the members prepared me for my new role. Robin made sure I was mentally prepared, Ty gave me the strength and belief that I needed, and the guards prepared my body physically. Without them, I have no doubt I'd already be dead. Maybe not by the hands of my own people, but certainly by one of the outsiders who saw the clan as an opening to advance themselves."

"Lee only wants those he handpicks to be strong, and everyone else he wants submissive. He'd do stupid shit to prove his power over us." She slipped her arms around his waist. "Lucy had long curly hair, just a couple shades darker than mine. I guess you could say it was more brown than red. Whenever she was reading, she'd wrap the strands around her fingers repeatedly. A few days after they mated, Lee forced her to cut it because he knew how much she liked it. Still, that wasn't enough for him and he took it a step further. They hadn't even been mated for a month and he shaved her head for disobeying him by speaking to Thorn and me."

"I'm sorry, sweetie."

"Her situation made me not want an Alpha for a mate. Hell, it made me not want a mate." She glanced up at him and saw kindness and sympathy in his eyes. "With you...I don't know, I want to believe it's different. Maybe I'm not the best judge, though, since I had hoped Lee would change when he found Lucy."

Her chest tightened at the thought of Lucy. What would have happened if she hadn't encouraged her sister to accept the mating? Denying a mate would mean either death or going rogue. Lucy felt suicide would free her from Lee, but Carleen talked her out of it. It was a guilt she would carry with her for the rest of her days. Nothing could change the past or make things right. She had made her choices and her sister now suffered the consequences.

"It's different and I'm going to show you." Placing his hands on her hips, he lifted her down to stand in front of him. "You were drawn into my flashback because I was touching you. I knew it was coming and I wanted to break contact but I couldn't. The hold was too strong and I dragged you into that. I'm sorry you witnessed the memory. Now that we know you're susceptible to it, I can show you something that will help you understand the type of Alpha I am. If you focus, you can control how the connection flows and see what you want."

"What?" She wasn't sure what to make of that word. It was almost like he was trying to say she had wanted it to happen, and she hadn't. She didn't even know it was possible.

"It's a rare talent even among Alphas, and still most people can't be dragged into it. The connection between the two needs to be strong. You're my mate, so there's no stronger connection."

"You could still hide things from me."

"What would be the point? Soon you'll know every part of my past and who I am. Lying to one's mate would make for an unhappy relationship." He leaned down, pressing his forehead against hers. "We've both spent too much time in darkness. Now, our future is going to be one full of happiness and sunshine."

Her body stilled as she stared into his eyes. The closeness between them had butterflies fluttering in her stomach—not out of nerves, but excitement. She wanted to know him better, and she also wanted more physically. "Why won't you kiss me?"

"Each time you've asked me, your tigress was lingering just under the surface. Your beast was controlling you. When I make you mine, I want it to be your decision, not your beast. I don't want you to regret it later." He caressed her arms, slowing working up toward her shoulders. "There's plenty of time."

"Really? Because I was told you're leaving the day after tomorrow." The idea of him not being there had her tiger snarling within her. They barely knew each other, yet she didn't want him to go. The future was uncertain, but for once in her life she wanted to roll with things. Just because Lee hadn't sought them out yet didn't mean that he wouldn't be an issue for her in the future. Thorn had been a valuable member of the guards, and she doubted Lee was willing to let him go without a fight. He'd want Thorn back even if it was just to prove a point. She knew it would be more than that. She and Thorn had been used to keep Lucy in her place, and it was unlikely Lee would be willing to lose the leverage he had over Lucy when it came to them.

Though Tex was an Alpha, it didn't mean he was anything like Lee. The Alaskan Tigers proved to her there were good Elders out there, and after everything Tex went through, he had to be one of the good ones. She couldn't see him running the clan like Lee or Avery had. There was a softness inside him. While he might keep that side of him hidden from others, he allowed her to see it.

"I have to return to Texas, but I'm hoping you'll come with me." He squeezed her shoulders. "I'm planning on offering Thorn a position. First, there's something he'll have to do."

She should have been ecstatic that her brother would get the position he wanted, but she wasn't sure. The possibility he'd discover she was destined to be with Tex before he got the position was too great. There was no doubt in her mind he wouldn't believe he'd gotten the position because of his own skill, but because of her.

She had told Tex the potential guards were celebrating, and while that was true for most of them, it wasn't for Thorn. He believed he had failed and the celebration was just an excuse to drown in his sorrows. The missed opportunity was something he'd certainly be kicking himself over, and nothing she might say would convince him otherwise.

Chapter Seven

Alone in the living room, Tex stood near the window with his third cup of coffee. It was after three in the morning and his time for sleep had passed without so much as a quick nap. After he'd walked Carleen home shortly after midnight, he tried to sleep but his mind refused to shut off. His thoughts were on her until he had to get up and go to the living room. He spent most of the last hour on the sofa just so he could breathe in her scent, which still lingered there.

For hours, they had sat there talking about everything from their past to what they wanted in the future. Never in his life had he shared so much with one person, but with her, it was easy. He wanted to know everything about her, and while he had been hesitant about telling her too much of his past, she had a way of putting him at ease, allowing him to reveal more than he had planned. Hours slipped past until it was well beyond midnight. It seemed liked minutes, but hours passed in the blink of an eye. He hadn't wanted her to go, but she needed to sleep and he had other things to deal with.

Before Rhett went to meet with Tad, they had put together a plan to test the first guard at three that morning. At that point, the plan sounded fine, but now Tex decided there needed to be a shakeup in the plans. Tex was used to going on very little sleep, so it had nothing to do with lack of sleep, and everything to do with proving Thorn had what it took to make it as part of the Elder Guards.

"Morning," Rhett called to him as he came out of the bedroom and headed straight for the kitchen and the pot of coffee.

"Just the person I wanted to see."

As he poured coffee, Rhett made a huffing sound as if he doubted it. "More like you were considering that cute redhead."

"Carleen." He eyed his guard, letting him know with his narrowed gaze that he wasn't amused he'd been checking her out.

"Hey, man, I thought jealousy wasn't something we had to deal with. Are you telling me they've lied about mating?" Rhett leaned against the kitchen counter, devouring his coffee. With every gulp, his eyes became more alert and his voice less of a growl.

"Not jealousy, more like protectiveness. She's been through a lot and I know you've got your doubts about Thorn, so I don't want you saying anything to upset her."

"I never said he couldn't do the job, I said he wasn't my first choice out of the others. You and Ben need Elder Guards more than anything. We need people who can help me train others. I'm not sure Thorn is cut out as an Elder Guard yet. He seemed to be allowing the hatred within him to eat him alive. There's also the issue that no one knows the reason behind him leaving Mississippi, not even Ty. Are you willing to invite someone into the clan who could be a security risk? Especially someone you're hoping to add as a guard?"

Tex wasn't surprised as Rhett polished off the coffee and turned to refill the mug. He was pretty sure Rhett had burned off enough layers from his tongue in the past to protect himself from the steaming hot liquid. "I don't think he's a security risk, but we'll make sure of it before we leave here. I think he's letting his state of mind influence him too much. He's concerned about the future. He feels Carleen is his responsibility. He forced her to leave Mississippi, and if he can't keep her safe then he's failed her just like he failed their sister, Lucy. I believe he's trying too hard and that's his issue. He went after Milo's shoulder thinking it would be a weakness and allowed him to win the fight without risking too much. He learned the hard way and he's beating himself up for it."

"They're a package deal, so you want him to do better in today's challenge."

"I don't want you to go light on him. Actually, just the opposite. I've decided we need to change the line-up. Thorn's first fight was weaker than Dawson's and Brody's, so I want him tested first." Tex glanced back out the window, over toward Carleen and Thorn's cabin. "I watched him stagger home under an hour ago. So, the timing is perfect."

"I saw the celebration they were having last night. Brody and Dawson were gone before I came back, but Thorn, a couple other guys, and some of the new guards who just arrived were still going at it. Thorn was already pretty hammered, so I can only imagine how bad he's feeling this morning. Have you considered the possibility he'll fail? What then?"

Tex considered it most of the night, but the fact remained the same. He needed to put Thorn through the worst test he could and go from there. If he failed, the position he had in mind wouldn't be his. If he was successful, there was no doubt that he wanted Rhett to work with him one-on-one until he was sure Thorn could handle it.

"Carleen is my mate and with her coming to Texas, it's likely Thorn will visit at the very least. If he's not chosen for a spot or doesn't accept it, he'll have the option to stay here and continue training, to hopefully be picked up by one of the other Alphas. Or he can return with us, as her brother and nothing more. He could work with the guards and we could see if there's a point in the future when he could take a position—whether that be guarding the grounds or guarding an Elder, I'm not sure."

"Have you spoken with her about this?" Rhett turned and placed his coffee mug in the sink.

He hadn't, but it didn't matter; their beasts wouldn't allow them to be apart for long. They would have to do something and from what she'd said hours before, she already accepted that. "I'll deal with it when the time comes. Now let's go."

Two hours had passed since Carleen overheard Tex and Rhett come retrieve Thorn for another session and with every minute that passed, she became more uneasy. Her brother had been drunk off his ass when he arrived back from the celebration, waking her from a dead sleep as he stumbled through the house, screaming her name. Tex's scent in the house angered him enough that he didn't care about keeping his voice down. He had been pissed that she agreed to have dinner with him and had voiced his displeasure before he left. She expected him to be gone for most of the night so she hadn't been worried about coming back early, yet it turned out that he had come back a little before eleven to apologize and she wasn't at the cabin.

He had considered going to Tex's cabin, but even in his drunken state he realized what a mistake it would be. Not only would it cost him the possible position with the Texas Tigers or any clan Ty had lined up, it would also force them to leave. Ty wouldn't accept Thorn's behavior and would have no choice but to force him to leave—which meant her, too. He had been sober enough to realize that would put them both in danger and that was the only reason he stopped himself before he could make a scene. He made it back to the celebration and with every drink, his anger grew. By the time he came home, he was livid and she was the only one there to deal with his rage.

What had happened in Mississippi to make Thorn so on edge? He hadn't been like that before. Not even when Lucy started to separate herself from them. Yet, something had changed and he was afraid. She just wasn't sure if he was afraid for both of them or just her. It didn't make sense that he was worried about her. She had kept herself out of the political aspects of the clan and did her best to keep herself hidden. The only time she came to Lee's attention was when Lucy pulled her aside and demanded that she gain control over her emotions. So, she couldn't comprehend his attitude.

She rubbed her temples, trying her best to push away the headache that had plagued her since her encounter with Thorn. Stress was not helping and neither had the hot bath she'd taken. A run would do wonders to relieve the tension, but it was out of the question until she knew what was going on. Whatever they wanted with Thorn could have their future in the balance. What was she going to do if he didn't make the guard roster? Tex told her that he was planning on offering him a position but there was something else he had to accomplish first. What if he didn't pass the second test? Could she leave him behind to go to Texas by herself?

If she was honest with herself, there was no other option. She had to go to Texas because that's where her mate had to be. His clan needed him and she accepted that. She just wasn't sure how it would affect things with Thorn or even what his backup plan was. He was so convinced he could secure a spot with the clan that he hadn't considered any other option. Without a backup plan and the results of his first test less than outstanding, he seemed to have lost his spark. There was no excitement in his eyes as he walked out the door to celebrate with the other guys. She had no doubt that he saw them leaving for Texas while he was stuck there waiting for the next Alpha.

The door flung open, startling her enough that she jumped. Warm tea sloshed over the rim of her mug and onto her hand. "Shit, Thorn, you..." It wasn't so much the look on his face as he entered, but Tex directly on his heels that stopped her from finishing her thought.

"We need to talk." Thorn marched toward her. "Alone."

"No." Before Thorn could reach her, Tex stepped in the way. "I told you to leave your anger at the door. You're going to behave rationally."

"What's going on?" She grabbed a napkin from the center of the round kitchen table and wiped her hands off before cleaning up the spilled tea.

"After everything you witnessed with Lucy, you're just going to fall into the arms of the first single Alpha. Are you insane, Carleen?" Thorn stepped back so he could see her around Tex. "Lucy wouldn't want that for you. She wouldn't want you to face the same fate she has."

"Are you trying to tell me I should be strong and take my own life? Because if you are, you're not the same brother I grew up with." Standing up from her chair, she tossed the damp napkin on the table and crossed her arms over her chest. "I was just thinking about how much you changed and now you're standing there proving me right. What the hell is going on with you?"

"Going on with me? What's going on with you? You completely ignored the fact I know you're Tex's mate."

"I'm not going to deny it, if that's what you mean. I planned to tell you. I just wanted to wait until after these tests. If you knew I was his mate, you'd have thought the only reason you got the position is because of me. You've worked so hard and I wanted you to get the position on your own. You're a strong guard and an excellent ally. You could prove yourself to Tex or any other clan you set your heart on."

"And he did." Rhett appeared in the still open doorway. "I hadn't planned on coming in. This is a family matter, but I needed to be close in case my assistance was required. Still, at that last comment, I couldn't stay quiet any longer. Thorn, I've made no attempt to hide that your first session didn't impress me. You went for what you considered Milo's weakness and it backfired."

"I know," Thorn snapped.

"Let him finish." Tex nodded to Rhett as if giving him the go-ahead.

"In the gym this morning, my impression changed. One-on-one, you surprised me. You revealed skills you didn't show during the first session. Even after a night of drink and little sleep, your fighting was clean. Instead of going after what you thought could be a weakness, you fought through it, waiting for your opening. Even after I blocked you twice, you kept with it until I gave you an opening. Every opponent is going to give you an opening and you've got to be ready to take it. Missing the opportunity could be the difference between life and death."

"I still wasn't able to take you down." Thorn shook his head, his disappointment in himself showing through his words.

"You're not connected to a strong Alpha or even a clan. When you renounced your commitment to Lee and the Mississippi Tigers, you cut that connection." Carleen tried to ease her brother's frustration and get him to see the larger picture.

"She's right." Tex reached back to take her hand in his and bring her to stand next to him. "The two of you are lone shifters and that makes you weaker than those connected to a clan with a strong Alpha leading them. Rhett's connection with me makes him stronger. You could have that, too, but if you continue to allow your anger to rule you, you're going to lose the opportunity."

"You expect—"

"Don't!" That single word came out as more of a shout than she had expected, but she knew what her brother was about to say and she had to stop him. "Thorn, please don't."

"Don't what, tell the truth? Voice my concern over your actions? Did you really except me to be quiet this time?" His gaze bored into her, making her stomach tighten, but she refused to back down.

"This is different and you know it. He isn't like Lee."

"How do you know?" Thorn snapped.

"Two reasons. Let's go with one you should have already realized." Taking her gaze away from Thorn, she glanced up at Tex and took in the man before her. Anyone who took a quick glance at him would assume he was in his early twenties, but what she saw in his eyes aged him. This man was her mate, and while he frightened her at first, the fear had dissipated. There was so much more to him than she realized at first and she was eager to know everything about him. The darkness in his past would surely come to light and while it helped to mold him into the man he was, it didn't define him. There was so much more to him and that was the side of him she wanted to know completely.

"Look at the hold he has over you." Thorn's rage tainted his voice, making his words come out in more of a growl. "You can't even finish your thought because you're too engrossed in him."

Shaking her head, she turned back to her brother. "There's no hold over me and that wasn't the reason I was looking at him. I got lost in my thoughts for a moment. The point is that you should realize he's not anything like Lee. I've come to know Ty, Tabitha, and many of the others here since we arrived and I know without a doubt that they'd never allow Tex here if they weren't completely sure he was on their side. You've worked with Ty and the others enough to know that, too."

"He could be hiding his true beliefs."

"Bullshit," Rhett snapped.

"He's right, you know." Instead of looking in Rhett's direction, she kept her attention on her brother. His shoulders seemed to relax and his fists were no longer clenched, making her wonder if they were getting through to him. "Tex has committed himself and his clan to Tabitha's cause. You know the legend as well as I do. Tabitha will be the strongest tigress ever born and once mated, the Queen of the Tigers and her King will grow stronger with each step they take to unite all tigers. There's no way Tex could hide a betrayal of that magnitude from them even if he wanted to."

"Maybe you're just defending him because you're his mate." The anger was gone and even as he tried to hold tight to his original stance, the conviction was gone from his tone. "Shit, Carleen, I'm just trying to keep you safe."

"She is safe," Tex replied before she could speak. "After what happened with Lucy, I understand your desire to protect her, but I'm not the one you need to shield her from."

"You're going to put her in more danger." Thorn stepped back toward the living room and sank down onto the accent chair. "You don't have the protection you need which is why you came here to find additional guards. With the resort set to open in the coming weeks, you're placing your clan in danger. After I learned about your clan, I thought you were the best fit. With some of the clan members living on the ninth floor, you've added safeguards to protect them. If I could convince you to give us, or at least Carleen, a room there, it would keep her safe. I could keep her safe and help you at the same time. It was a win-win for everyone."

"Then you should be happy to know the precautions taken for the tenth floor, the Elders floor, went even further. As my mate, Carleen will reside there." Still holding her hand, he led her toward the sofa so they could continue the conversation in comfort. "While the work isn't complete yet, the suites have been opened up to provide us larger living quarters. There will be extremely limited access to this floor. Out of six permanent living quarters, only three are occupied. In addition to those, there are six guest suites on the floor, and a private meeting room. Those with permanent quarters on the floor include me, my Lieutenant, Ben Evans, and Rhett. The additional ones are for future Captains of the Guards for both Ben, his future mate, and my mate."

"With the danger level of guest suites on your private floor being so high, I cannot believe you'd allow that." Thorn's statement was directed at Tex but his gaze was on her, as if telling her to reconsider her actions.

"One is for the West Virginia Tigers' Alpha, Jinx. His mate, Summer, is Ben's sister and their adopted daughter Claire was born in my clan. Claire's situation is a long story that isn't important at the moment. They have a guest suite for their visits and there's room for a couple guards. These suites will also be used if Ty and Tabitha visit, as their protection is of the utmost importance."

"The eighth floor is also undergoing renovations to provide enhanced security measures to other Elders of committed clans," Rhett explained from his position near the now closed door. "Before all of this started, you have to remember a couple years ago when Manetka Resort was the place to be for shifters. We're hoping to bring that back safely, without jeopardizing the Elders or the clan. Every reservation will be going through security checks to ensure that we're not allowing our enemies into the resort. Manetka will be a safe place where those fleeing Alphas like Lee can go."

"That doesn't sidestep the fact Carleen will be in more danger because of you. All I've wanted to do was keep her safe, and now look at this. Damn it, she's all I have left." Thorn ran his hand through his hair. "Lee's not going to like it when he finds out."

At the mention of Lee, her heart skipped a beat and it was as if the moment froze. All she could think about was Lucy. Her sister would suffer for Carleen's mating with Tex. Every move she made, every comment spoken, always reflected on Lucy. *Why did I think that would change when we left Mississippi?*

Chapter Eight

Everything in Tex encouraged him to protect his mate from Thorn's anger, but Carleen would not have appreciated him sheltering her. The conversation had to happen and it was better to have it out in the open before things went any further. He needed to know what Thorn truly felt about not only the mating, but also about him as an Alpha. It could be seen as one final test for the potential guard, but he perceived it as a glance into Thorn's mind before he accepted him into the Texas Tigers.

"Sweetie? You okay?" As she shivered, he wrapped his arm around her shoulders and brought her back against his body.

"I…fi…" She shook her head. "Oh, shit. Thorn…Lucy…he's going to hurt her."

"What are you talking about?" Tex turned her to face him. "Who's going to hurt her? Me?" The only answer she gave was a shake of her head as she fought back the tears.

"She's talking about Lee." Thorn let out a grunt and leaned forward to place his hand on his sister's knee. "There's nothing we can do, Car. We don't even know what happened after we left."

"It's been a long time since you've called me Car."

"I know." Thorn lifted his hand off her leg and leaned back against the chair. "It seems like a lifetime ago."

"Carleen." Tex called her name, hoping to bring her attention back to him and away from the past. "Give me a little time. I'll see what I can do to help her. Don't lose hope."

"Hope…" She let out a light chuckle. "It's already gone. I know what her fate will be."

"What do you mean?" He rubbed his hand along her back, trying his best to comfort her. Without the mating connection complete, there was only so much he could do.

"You said it yourself. Lee can't be left in control over the Mississippi Tigers, which means he'll be killed. When he dies, he'll pull Lucy down with him. She's not strong enough to survive that. He's broken her will and her spirit."

"Rhett, go find out what Ty's morning is like. I need to meet with him on an urgent matter." He caressed the small of her back with his fingertips. "There might be nothing I can do, but I'm going to try."

"Tex." Rhett's hand was wrapped around the door handle as he looked back at him. "About before…I disagreed with you then, but you were right."

"I'll take care of it." He waited until the door was shut behind Rhett before looking over at Thorn. "You've proven a lot this morning but there are still things we need to discuss."

"Let's do it."

"Carleen, why don't you lie down for a bit? You're exhausted." He pulled her tight against him. "Worrying isn't going to change whatever the future holds."

"He's right. You need some sleep. We lost Lucy a long time ago and even if we *can* save her from Lee, she's not going to be the same."

She pulled out of his embrace and turned to her brother. "She's our sister."

"I'm very much aware of that. I'm just remembering what Lucy's mating did to our father. Mom was optimistic, but Dad knew Lee hadn't changed. In the end, it broke something in Mom and now she's dead."

"She was killed in an accident."

"No, Carleen…Mom left the safety of the house, hoping to die. Without batting an eye, she walked right into the gunfire and straight toward the shooters. Dad was too far away to do anything and the other guards on duty were busy returning fire. They were defending our clan and no one was able to stop her." He dragged his hand over his face and pinched the bridge of his nose. "Unable to do anything, I watched from the window as it happened."

"Why?" Her sorrow thickened the air as the first tear rolled down her check. "Why didn't you do something? Why didn't Dad? He had to know she was depressed. Hell, I knew."

"Before Dad left, he ordered me to stay with you and Mom. I couldn't leave you and even if I could, there were two men outside our window, creeping toward Lee's house. I'd have never made it to Mom before they saw me. My only hope was Dad or another guard intervening." He leaned forward, resting his elbows on his knees. "There might not have been love between them, but he didn't want to see her depressed like she was. He tried to help but nothing worked. He got to the point where he didn't know what to do for her."

"Lee's taken so much from our family, so much from the clan. Whatever the cost, he's got to be stopped. He can't continue to ruin lives."

"I'm going to talk to Ty soon and we'll put together a plan if he doesn't already have one," Tex assured her. He wasn't certain what would become of her father or Lucy, but Lee had to be a priority. He might not be torturing members like Avery had, but he was still controlling them. More than that, Lee was a threat to Tabitha and all tiger shifters.

"There's no way I'm going to be able to sleep, so I'm going to go shower and let you two talk." She rose from the sofa and started to step around his legs when he grabbed hold of her hand.

"Sweetie, you're welcome to stay. I only suggested sleep because I know you were up when we came to get Thorn. When I touch you, I know you haven't been sleeping well. Your tigress is growing irritable." His thumb teased over her wrist. "Come sit back down."

"It's fine. I'll let you two talk. But could I have a minute alone with you first?"

"I'll go," Thorn offered.

"No." She watched Tex as he stood. "We'll go back to my room. It will only be a minute."

Tex interlaced their fingers as they headed back to her room. They barely knew each other but the simple act of holding hands made him forget that. When they touched, it was as if they had known each other their whole lives, and their beasts became one. This was what every shifter waited for and now he had it. His mate was right there in front of him and while his tiger was urging him to claim her, he knew once he did she'd be in danger. The clan had come a long way, but adding new guards and opening the resort again would be stressful on all of them. Bringing his mate home would no doubt add additional complications and stress. He needed to make sure she was protected and that meant he needed to assign a Captain of the Guards for her, at the very least.

"Tex?"

"Yeah…" Shoving his thoughts aside, he realized she was standing in front of him and they were in her bedroom. The space was the same as his, all the way down to the deep blue comforter on the bed. The only difference was the framed family photo sitting on the stand next to the bed. Something about how it was angled toward the bed told him that if he could see the photograph, it would show her family together—before Lucy mated. A happier time. "What did you want to talk about?"

"Everything between us is happening so quickly, making me uncertain of things, but I have to make sure you're not giving Thorn a position because of me. If he isn't up for what you need, then you're not only risking his life and your clan, but you're risking your life, and I can't stand by while that happens." She slipped her hand out of his and stepped back.

"Get back here." He reached out and wrapped his arms around her waist, pulling her flush against the front of his body. "If he wasn't up for the task, I wouldn't risk your life by making him the Captain of your Guards."

"What?" Her eyes widened as she stared up at him.

"I haven't claimed you yet, but I'm hoping you'll allow me that privilege before we return to Texas. You'd go in as Alpha Female with the protection you deserve. It's going to take some time to complete your guard team, but at least you'll have him to protect you when I can't be with you."

"I don't understand. Why did you choose Thorn? I know we're close, but it seems odd that you'd choose him when Rhett wasn't even sure he was good enough to make the cut."

"He told me why you left." His hands slid under her shirt and up the sides of her body. "Do you realize how much I want to push you down on that bed and strip these clothes off you?"

"Focus." She placed her hands on his forearms, stopping him from rubbing any higher. "Why did he tell you? How could he do that? I don't even know what happened to force us to leave in the middle of the night."

Her words had his hands stilling and he leaned back enough to look at her to ensure she was serious. "Peaches?"

"I can't believe him!" She shook her head, sending a strand of her red hair into her eyes. "He came to me in the middle of the night and forced me to leave without an explanation. Even months later, he still hasn't told me, but you've known him for two days and he tells you. What the hell?"

"He was trying to protect you."

"From what?" Her voice raised a notch.

As she fought to keep control over her emotions, he led her farther into the room to sit on the bed. "He was protecting you from Lee and leaving was the only option."

"From Lee? What the hell is that supposed to mean? Why would—"

"Because Lucy tried to sneak off to see you." At the sound of Thorn's voice, they both turned to find him standing in the doorway. "This place is too small for me not to hear when you're yelling, Car."

"I was handling it," Tex told him as Thorn leaned against the doorframe.

"I know, but her anger shouldn't be directed at you. If she wants to be pissed at someone, then I'm that person." His gaze drifted toward her. "Lee was hollering at Lucy earlier that night but it wasn't until my shift was nearly over when I heard him order two guards to bring you to him. He wanted you dead so that the temptation of Lucy going to see you was gone."

"He planned to kill me?"

Thorn nodded. "Dad told me to get you and run. He couldn't come with us but he wanted you to be safe. It was a lose-lose situation and I did the only thing I could. I got you and we left. It was the only way to keep you alive."

"At what cost?" Her voice broke, but she held it together.

"We don't know." Tex held her against him. "Little information is available on the status of the Mississippi Tigers. Ty has a group near the area with the hopes of learning more before they need to make their move."

"There's nothing we can do for any of them. If we make a move on Lee, he'll kill Lucy for it. Dad entrusted your safety to me and that's my priority. If he can save Lucy, he will," Thorn reasoned.

"I can't handle any more right now. Please...I just need some time. I want to be alone."

"Whenever you're ready, Tex, I'll be in the living room." Thorn turned and headed back the way he'd come.

She had asked to be alone, but she clung to Tex's hand. The minutes ticked by as they silently sat there, his arm around her waist and his other hand in hers. "Are you okay?"

She let out a deep breath. "Honestly, I don't know. Lee has murdered others for disobeying him, but to know he wanted me dead when I tried to stay out of his way is unsettling. I did everything I could to avoid getting Lucy in trouble with him but in the end...if Thorn hadn't overheard the orders, I'd have been killed."

"You're alive and that's what matters right now." He leaned in closer, pressing his check to the top of her head. "Let me worry about dealing with Lee."

"I know we're not mated yet, so I have no right but..." Biting her lip, she trailed off, obviously uneasy.

"No right to what?" He lifted his head and used his thumb to tilt her head back enough for him to look at her.

"When you go speak with Ty, can I come? I need him to know about Lucy and I need to know what he's planning. Please, Tex."

"Shh, sweetie. You can come. I can't promise you can stay for our whole meeting, but you can come and say what you need to." His chest tightened with the knowledge that they probably wouldn't be able to save Lucy. They could try, but at least part of it would be up to her in the end. She had to be willing to live without her mate and if her spirit was as broken as Carleen believed it to be, it was unlikely she'd be strong enough.

Death and destruction had been the highlights of his life, along with the torture Avery had dished out to nearly every member of the clan. Now that he was Alpha, he wanted to change that. He wanted his life to be filled with something other than horrors. He wanted his clan to have a safe place where they were happy. Since Carleen came into his life, he was wondering if that was even possible. Once they eliminated Elders killing their members, they'd have to deal with humans trying to kill them. There would always be something.

"My brother is a stubborn mule, but his temper isn't always this bad. He's just testy because he doesn't like change and the uncertainty is bothering him. Even seeing the worst in him, you're willing to give him a position within your clan, and that means the world to me."

"Not just any position. He's going to oversee the protection of the most valuable person in my life. That's an honor, and I'll kill him if he lets anything happen to you." He waited for her to say something, but she remained silent. "He's protected you before and I know he'll keep you safe in the future. Most shifters don't have a strong connection with their families but you have one with Thorn and that's going to make the job personal for him. He'll want to protect you, not because you're the Alpha's mate and his life would be hell if something happened to you, but because you matter to him, too."

"Shouldn't you wait to ask him until…"

"I want you protected and if Thorn won't do it, then I need to find someone else. If he will, then I want him to go through another session with Styx and Felix before we leave. He'll be guarding the Alpha Female of the clan, which adds additional threats into the mix. They can prepare him for that."

"Tex!" Rhett hollered moments before the front door slammed shut. "Where are you?"

"Back here." He rose from the bed to stand slightly in front of her. He wasn't worried Rhett would hurt her but the tone of his voice was enough to put Tex on guard. When his guard appeared in the doorway, he took the man in. "What's going on?"

"You need to come with me. Now. You too, Carleen." Rhett glanced at Carleen, and Tex watched as his eyes softened. There was a touch of sadness in his face that hadn't been there before. "Ty's waiting. Let's go."

"What happened?" Tex pressed again, since Rhett hadn't answered him the first time.

"It's the Mississippi Tigers. I don't know all the details, I was just sent to get you." Rhett turned and headed back the way he came.

"Come on." Tex slipped his arm around her waist and pulled her against him until her body brushed along his.

"Thorn," she called to him as they were making their way out of the room.

"I'm here." He stood near the door, his face drawn and pale. "We don't know anything yet. Maybe Lee's had a change of heart and will support Tabitha."

"That's the same hope I had before the mating. Now I know he can never change. He's doomed and so is Lucy. Maybe we all are."

"Have faith, sis."

"How about we all just go find out what's happening?" Rhett stood next to the open front door. "It's the only way you're going to know and speculating will just waste time."

Tex led Carleen past the other two men and headed straight for the main building where Ty's quarters were. Clan members moved around the area, many of them working construction as they finalized the second-floor addition. Soon the Elders would have their own floor with the Captains of their Guards, giving Tabitha extra protection in case of an attack on the compound.

"Remember what it was like to be young, without a care in the world?" She tipped her head toward the far side of the main building. "For shifter children, their innocent years end earlier than humans, but while they last they're carefree."

The schoolhouse stood hidden from view of the perimeter, where some of the clan children headed in for their morning class. It reminded him of yet another thing he needed to establish back in Texas. There weren't any school-aged children in the clan now, but they'd have some in the future, either through new members joining or those already there. Soon they'd be raising the next generation of the Texas Tigers. He needed to be prepared for that.

"I can't remember what it was like to be carefree. Avery killed my parents before I was old enough to remember them. One of the single tigresses took me in and Avery had me doing odd jobs for him. By the time I was fifteen, he had me working as a guard." With one final glance at the children, he grabbed the door handle, opened it, and ushered her inside. "Unlike those children, I was never allowed to attend school. Avery tried to mold me into what he wanted, the perfect guard, but I wouldn't give him that satisfaction. The tigress who took me in was the clan's school teacher and taught me at night so that I would still get the education I needed, even though Avery had me training with the guards during the day."

"I'm sorry." She halted, Thorn and Rhett stopping behind her. "Your childhood was robbed from you."

"It prepared me for where I am now." With his arm around her waist, he tugged her forward. "I fought against what he was trying to do by pretending to be weaker than I was, but I remember everything they taught me and that's keeping me alive now. It also showed me the kind of Alpha I *didn't* want to be. I don't want people to follow me out of pity, but out of respect."

"I hate to break up your bonding moment, but can we get moving?" Thorn bitched. "I want to know what's happening to Lucy and Dad."

"We're here." Tex tipped his head toward Adam who was standing outside the door to Ty's quarters. "Whatever we learn, we'll handle it *together*."

Whatever Ty had to tell them wouldn't be good news, and Carleen already expected the worst, making him want to protect her from it. Touching her was only showing him part of her emotions, making him wish he'd claimed her. He needed to know what was going on within her. If their mating had been official, he could help her through this better. Instead, he felt as if he'd been watching her from behind a wall and there was little he could do. He hadn't felt this helpless since Adam brought him to Alaska and he knew the rest of the clan was suffering while he was safe. He hadn't been able to save them, but he'd do everything he could to protect Carleen and those she cared about.

Chapter Nine

Everywhere around Carleen, the day was moving on as if nothing had happened. It wasn't that they didn't care; they just didn't know. It wouldn't be long before the word spread, but for now the news had been confined to the Elders, a couple of their guards, Thorn, Tex, and her. She was supposed to meet Brooklynn and Mira for lunch but she wasn't in the mood now. With her heart shattered and grief pouring through her, she didn't have the strength to pretend everything was fine. Tex had tried to comfort her, but she needed to be alone. Sitting there surrounded by the Elders, she couldn't let out her emotions. She had to control them unless she wanted everyone in the room to feel what was going on within her.

All she needed was a short break to get control over her grief and then she could go back. Maybe by then they'd learn something new. She wasn't holding out hope that Lucy had survived, but she wanted to hear what they'd found. There were others in Mississippi she cared about, and she needed to know their fate.

Barely aware of her surroundings, she stepped up onto the deck of the cabin, and as she wrapped her hand around the door handle, she caught a movement out of the corner of her eye. "What the hell?"

"It's only us." Mira rose from the chair to stand with Brooklynn who had been leaning against the railing. "We thought we'd bring lunch to you."

"I'm sorry…I'm not really in the mood." She stared at the two women and realized for the first time she'd made friends who weren't related to her.

The quick friendship that developed between the three of them was stronger than any other friendship she had, including her relationship with Lucy. She could tell them anything, but as she stood there, she didn't know how to tell them what was happening.

"Carran told me." Brooklynn stepped away from the railing and came closer. "He wanted me to know so we wouldn't expect you for lunch. Carleen, I'm sorry, I really am. I want you to know if there's anything you need, all you have to do is ask. We're here for you. We understand if you'd rather be alone. At least take this. You and Thorn can have it for dinner." She held out the basket, but Carleen made no move to take it.

"She did it. She let them in." Her voice broke as anguish rushed through her, making her legs weak. "Lee was becoming dangerous and she knew he needed to be stopped. Dad had the connections, but they needed a way in— they needed her. Even knowing what it would cost, she gave them that."

"Let's get you inside." Mira came to her and put her arm around her shoulders. "Ty, Tex, and everyone else is doing everything they can."

"I know." In a fog, she let Mira help her into the house. "Ty gave the team orders to move in, but it was too late. The damage was done. Tex and Thorn are still with Ty. I couldn't take any more. I needed a break."

"I'm still putting together my team, but if we can be of any help Ty knows we're available." Inside, Brooklynn placed the basket of food on the small coffee table in front of the sofa. "I know you want to be alone, but it would be the worst thing for you right now. Your beast needs the connection with others, especially since you're not committed to a clan yet. Another tigress would offer more to you than I can. Do you want me to call Kallie, Harmony, or even Tara?"

"No, I'm fine." Knowing they were right, she sank down on the sofa, positioning herself in the middle so they'd be on either side of her. Just being near them, the rough edge of her emotional state began wearing down and she could breathe again. The tension hanging in the air dissipated—unlike when she'd been with the Elders—reminding her that she needed to stay in control. In the cabin with Mira and Brooklynn, she could allow herself freedom of emotions.

"You're sure learning a lot about us and quick." She glanced at Brooklynn, surprised that as a human she was already well in tune with what shifters needed. "Years ago, I knew a human who had been mated to a shifter for years and she still didn't understand what our kind needed. She felt what her mate needed, but she didn't understand it."

"With mates it's easier. Shifter or human, they'll be in tune with what their mate needs and will be able to provide that comfort even if it's unusual to them. But this will be so much more than that." Brooklynn sat down next to Carleen, close enough that their shoulders touched. "Heading Shifter Peace Keepers, I need to understand things that human mates might not. I must understand what the Elders need in order to get my team out alive. Understanding what the shifter in front of me is feeling and catching the vibes he's putting off will not only allow me to get to the issue at hand, it will make sure we walk away from the encounter."

"You'll be going into dangerous situations. Anything could happen." Her mind started playing out images of what could have occurred if Brooklynn's team came to Mississippi. Lee would have had a fit and there wasn't a doubt in her mind someone would have gotten hurt, or even died. Instead of the Shifter Peace Keepers invading the Mississippi Tigers, it was someone else. Still, the results would be the same. How many died because of this attempt to overthrow Lee and free the clan?

"Trust me, Styx and the others are preparing her for it." Mira sat next to her and began to dig through the basket. "He's working her harder than anyone I've seen him train."

"I have the bruises to prove it." Brooklynn gave a light laugh before growing serious again. "I wouldn't have it any other way. I have to be ready to face whatever comes our way and I need my team to know I can handle myself. I might not be a shifter, but if I'm going to lead them I have to be just as powerful as one or they'll never respect me."

"Along with training, Carran is working with her to sense what's happening around her." Mira unloaded the containers of food onto the coffee table and set the basket aside. "If she goes to a clan that isn't committed to Tabitha, she'll have no connection to the Elders and will be essentially blind if she's just relying on that. She'll have to focus on the scents in the air, body language, and the hidden meanings behind their words."

Brooklynn had her work cut out for her when it came to Shifter Peace Keepers, but Carleen believed she'd be successful. It wasn't all the hours she had trained or her years of being a police officer before Carran found her, it was Brooklynn's drive. In the weeks she'd been in Alaska, Carleen watched as Brooklynn became stronger and more comfortable in what she was doing. As Carran's mate, she grew in strength and other abilities. While it wasn't supposed to be the same as what a shifter could accomplish, she was making it work for her. She'd come further than anyone else Carleen had known. Even Carran was impressed.

"Next week, we're going to meet with a couple people about joining the team. Once the team is assembled and structured, we can begin training together. Those here who are part of the crew have already begun their training," Brooklynn explained as Mira handed her a plate. "It's taken longer than I expected to get to this point, but before we brought others on board I wanted Carran to get comfortable with the idea of me going out there without him."

"Has he?"

"Let's just say it's better than I expected." Brooklynn glanced around her to Mira. "Hasn't he?"

"Carran will be fine. They're mates, so it's common to be worried. His natural reaction is to protect her and he's not going to be there. That's why Ty's been working with her to shield Carran."

"Not completely shield him." Brooklynn shook her head. "It's a balancing act that I'm trying to get a handle on. If I block him too much it affects him to a point that he can't focus on his own work because his beast is too fixated on me and the lack of a connection. If I don't shield him, he's going to think I'm in danger when I might just be uncomfortable. The distance isn't going to make it easier, so we've already scheduled a test run."

"I brought hot cocoa, which I know you love since you discovered the kitchen staff makes it with real chocolate...none of that powdered stuff. But I also have wine. Though it's early, I think it might be the better choice."

"Wine. I'm not much of a drinker, but I need this today." She placed her plate on her lap and took the bottle from Mira. Reading the label, her chest tightened. "This is Lucy's favorite. In honor of her, let's crack this baby open and celebrate her life. You didn't know her, but she was an amazing big sister."

"You're sure she's..." Brooklynn's words trailed off and she shook her head. "I'm sorry."

"No official word has come through, but I just know." She ran her hand over the label and forced herself to swallow past the lump forming in the back of her throat. "Lee broke her will to a point that she won't be able to survive his death. I should be happy she's finally free of him, but I'm selfish and want her to be alive."

"It's not selfish." Mira took the bottle from her and grabbed the bottle opener. "From what you told us it sounds like she sacrificed herself so that others could have freedom from him. She was courageous and she'd wanted you to remember that. Don't let yourself dwell on the negativity. Focus on the positives. Cherish the wonderful times you had with her and as long as she lives on in your memories and stories, she'll never be forgotten."

"Everyone she saved today will always remember her sacrifice." Brooklynn squeezed her hand. "She'll live on forever through them and their children."

You'll never be forgotten, Lucy. I miss you so much already.

Standing in Ty's living room, Tex debated about going after Carleen. The only thing that kept him rooted in place was the promise of a call from the team in Mississippi. As much as he wanted to be with his mate, he needed to know what they'd found. Each minute passed slower than the last, making his tiger pace within him. The constant growl from his beast repeating the same thing over and over only served to put him on edge. *Go to her, go to her, go to her now!*

"Take this." Ty handed him one of the untraceable cell phones. "I'll patch you in on the call when it comes through. Go to your—" Ringing from the phone strapped to Ty's belt cut him off and sent relief rushing through Tex.

"Finally."

Ty set the second phone aside before pulling his phone off his belt and hitting a couple buttons. "Hello."

"It's over." Mason's voice came through the speakerphone, allowing everyone in the room to hear the update. "We'll stick around to assist with the cleanup and meet with the new Alpha once he's had a moment to process what's happened."

"You're confirming Lee is dead then?" Ty asked.

"What about Lucy?" Tex demanded, needing to know for Carleen's sake. "The clan's Alpha Female."

"I can confirm the following: The former Alpha, Lee, has been killed. Jack has taken over the position of Alpha, and Lucy was not killed in the struggle. However..." Mason paused as if searching for the correct words. "Carleen and Thorn, I apologize to have to give you such news over the phone, but Lucy is also deceased. She took her own life."

"Bullshit!" Thorn screamed. "Lee killed her."

"Enough!" Ty shot Thorn a warning glance. "Are you sure of that, Mason?"

"We arrived when Jack and Lee were entangled in a fight. Lee had razorblades between his claws, allowing him to slice deeper and draw more blood with every swing. I believe she knew her father would die and that everything they had done would be for nothing. If Lee had lived, he'd have killed her for allowing Jack and the others in. She did the only thing she could. She took her life to weaken him enough that Jack could put an end to his reign."

Tex had the information he needed and instead of waiting for Ty and Mason to wrap up the conversation, he headed for the door. He had to get to Carleen. Her pain was like a knife in his chest and the news he was about to deliver would only make it worse, but she had to know what they'd learned.

In an all-out run, he crossed the compound heading straight for where he knew she would be, barely aware that Rhett was jogging behind him and trying to catch up. His guard's annoyance was barely more than a caress along Tex's otherwise occupied tiger. He climbed the steps and without knocking, he opened the door. Before he could enter, the sound of the woman drifted toward him, stopping him in his tracks.

"To sisters, both biological and those we choose," Brooklynn declared as the sound of glasses clinking drifted toward him.

"To Lucy," Mira added.

"She'd scold us for having wine at lunch instead of with a fancy dinner. She always said a good wine should be enjoyed either with a delicious dinner or with noteworthy friends." The sadness lacing Carleen's voice had him stepping through the door and into view.

"And to celebrate one's life." He came around the half wall to stand next to the sofa. "We must never forget those who touch our lives, otherwise they're truly gone."

"She's dead, isn't she?" With tears in her eyes, she looked up at him.

"Come here, baby." He held his hand out to her. When she took it, he pulled her up off the sofa, past Mira, and into his arms. "Excuse us." He didn't even glance back at the other women as he led her back to her bedroom. While he wanted to pick her up and take her to his cabin, so they could be alone, he held off.

"What did you find out?"

"Inside." He ushered her in before closing the door behind them.

"She's dead." It was no longer a question as she dropped down onto the bed. "I knew it."

"I'm sorry, Carleen." He stood in front of her, debating whether he should sit down next to her or remain standing. In the end, it was her who made the decision.

"Hold me."

"Always, sweetie." He went around the other side of the bed and without pulling the covers down, he climbed on, lying flat on his back. "Come here."

"What are you planning?" She eyed him suspiciously.

"You asked me to hold you, so come here. Nothing will happen that you don't want to happen." Reaching over to her, he caressed her forearm with his fingers. "Actually, nothing's going to happen. I stretched out hoping you'd be able to get some sleep. Now, come here. I can feel your pain. Let me do what little I can to help ease the burden."

"Tell me what happened." She kicked off her shoes and crawled over to cuddle next to him.

"We already suspected your father led a group to take down Lee for good and that Lucy let them in. Mason confirmed that. She was alive when Ty ordered the team to go in."

"I don't know Mason. Is he part of the clan?" She tucked her head against him, and draped her arm over his chest.

"Mason is the Alpha of the Arizona Tigers. His clan was attacked several months ago. They've been rebuilding their compound and since most of the clan was killed in the attack, Mason has been working on growing his clan. In the next few months, he should be able to return to Arizona full-time but until then, he's been staying here at least part-time. For the last several weeks, he's been away from the compound which is why you haven't met him yet. He was in Texas when Ty started to put together a team for the Mississippi mission."

"I remember that. Randolph ordered the attack and most of the clan was murdered. I didn't know the Alpha's name, but I remember the Captain of his Guards abandoning him."

"Due to a family issue he couldn't handle, Chad left after they got to safety. Now Mason has a new Captain, Spencer, who was part of the Alaskan Tigers before taking his new position. Mason is protected and with Spencer by his side, he led the team in Mississippi." Rubbing his hand along her back, he realized she wasn't going to ask what happened. He wasn't sure if that was because she didn't want to know or because asking would confirm what she feared. "Mason spoke with your sister—"

"Lee killed her, didn't he?"

"No. Jack and Lee were entangled in a fight for dominance. Lee had razorblades between his claws and with every blow he landed, your father bled more. Jack challenged Lee for the clan, and even though the team was there, they could do nothing but allow the battle to play out. Afterward, they could kill Lee if he was the survivor. Wanting to get Lucy somewhere safe, Mason reached for her to force her back toward Spencer, but it was already too late." He wrapped his arm around her, snuggling her closer to his side. "She realized Jack was going to die if something didn't change, and I don't think she realized that Mason and the others were there to kill Lee. She knew if Lee survived that he'd kill her for allowing Jack's men in, so she did the only thing she could think of. She took her life to weaken him enough that your father could put an end to the battle."

"No!" Her scream came out on a sob and tears rolled down her cheeks.

"I'm so sorry, Carleen." He pressed his lips to the top of her head, wishing he could do something to ease her pain. Seeing his mate cry was far worse than feeling her emotions burning within him. He wanted to do something to make this right, but there was nothing he could do. He couldn't bring back the dead. Even if he could, the very fact that Lucy had been able to weaken Lee as much as she had with her own death was proof that their beasts were deeply connected. She never would have survived Lee's execution, and after his latest threats against Tabitha, they could do nothing else but eliminate him.

Chapter Ten

Waking up in bed alone, Carleen grabbed the pillow Tex had been using and pulled it close. His spicy scent of dry cedar and vanilla lingered, making her press her nose into the pillow and take a deep breath. His scent eased the anxiety and loss within her, making it easier to breathe. In the moments when her emotions wanted to drown her, he was her life preserver, keeping her afloat.

That very thought made her realize she'd found him at the right time. She needed him now more than ever. A knot formed in her stomach from fear of the unknown. He was an Alpha and once they completed the mating, it would cement things between them, putting her in the same position Lucy had been in. Everything she learned about Tex showed her he was nothing like Lee, but that fear remained.

He had pulled her into his flashback before and offered to do it again, allowing her to see more of him. Yet, she hadn't taken his offer, partly because she was terrified of what she might find, while the other part of her wanted to learn it as it came. They were supposed to be on this journey together. She could be pulled into his flashbacks, but she had nothing to offer him. He'd have to wait until their mating to know what kind of person she was. That didn't seem right and instead of taking him up on his offer, she forced herself to trust those around her. Ty trusted Tex and she trusted Ty. That had to be enough.

"Carleen?"

The whisper from the other side of the door had her bolting upright with the pillow still clutched in her hand. The scent outside was familiar enough that she could tell the visitor was human, but tied to the clan. It was the hint of something else within the aroma of human and tigers that kept her on high alert. "Who's there?"

"It's Courtney."

"Come in." Relieved, she dropped the pillow back onto the bed. Courtney's scent was mixed with her mates, which explained the lingering bear scent clinging to her from her second mate, Thaddeus.

The door pushed open and Courtney stepped into the room. "I didn't want to wake you but…"

"It's fine. What's going on? What are you doing here? Where's Tex?"

"Tex didn't want to leave you alone, but he had to go meet with Ty, so I offered to stay with you. Milo's here, too, in the living room." She shifted from one foot to the other. "Mason's here and he wants to speak with you."

"Mason?" She took a deep breath and nodded. "Okay, give me a minute and I'll be out."

"Tex is on his way back over, too." Courtney turned back to the door. "I heard what happened in Mississippi…if you need anything, I'm here."

"Thanks." She scooted to the edge of the bed and waited until Courtney left before standing.

Her thoughts raced through her mind faster than she could keep up with them. What did Mason want? Tex told her that he was staying in Alaska while his compound was being rebuilt in Arizona, but that didn't explain why he'd decided to visit her. She wanted a shower, but refused to take the time. After a quick glance in the mirror, she dragged her hand through her hair, fluffing it the best she could and headed out.

"Where is she?" Tex's voice carried back to her room as the front door banged close behind him.

"I'm here." She stepped into the small hallway and her gaze found Tex. Concern darkened his eyes as he made his way toward her. "What's wrong?"

"Nothing, peaches." When he was close enough to touch her, he wrapped his arms around her waist, bringing her against the front of his body. "I just wanted to be with you when Mason spoke with you. I was worried I wouldn't make it in time."

"If I had known, I would have waited." Another male voice spoke and she could only assume it was Mason.

"We'll be leaving now, but if you need anything, Carleen, let me know."

Over Tex's shoulder, she caught a glimpse of Courtney and Milo moving toward the door, but her attention was on her mate. "You're here now. That's what matters."

"Now and always." He interlaced their fingers. "Come on, let's not keep Mason waiting any longer. He's had a long trip and is no doubt tired."

"I've rushed back to Alaska as fast as Thaddeus could get me here, because what I have to say couldn't wait and needed to be delivered in person." Mason set a glass of what appeared to be water aside and rose. "Please, come sit. I only need a few minutes of your time."

"I don't understand. What is this about?" Needing the comfort Tex could offer, she stayed close to him as they entered the living room, heading straight for the sofa. Unlike before when she was uneasy just from standing in front of an Elder, it was the impending conversation making her anxious. He had been with her sister in the final minutes of her life and there was no doubt that whatever brought him to her cabin had to do with that.

"Lucy." Mason waited for her to sit before taking a seat on the chair across from them. "I spoke with your sister before she died."

"I know. Tex told me she…" Her voice cracked, forcing her to take a deep breath and swallow. "She took her own life."

"I was checking to see that she was okay when the commotion from Jack and Lee drew my attention. I only looked away for a second." He shook his head. "I never saw the gun in her hand until it was too late and I'm sorry for that. Ty informed me Lucy's will had been broken, making the connection she had with Lee stronger. Still, I wanted to get her out of there safely. We were going to take care of Lee, but after speaking with Ty we thought we might be able to save her from dying alongside him."

"How?" She glanced at Tex. "I know you tried to hide it, but I felt your concern when I told you her will was broken. You knew she'd die."

"That was before I spoke with Ty and Tabitha."

"Let me explain." Mason leaned forward. "It's purely hypothetical since we were unable to test it, but Tabitha believed that an Elder might have been able to pull her from the connection she had with Lee. In order to do that, we would have had to be there before he was killed or at the very least arrive before she lost consciousness. His death would break the hold he had over her and to save her, she'd need to find someone else strong enough to keep her will alive and force her to fight."

"We weren't sure if Mason would be enough. He doesn't have a large clan behind him anymore, but he's a strong Alpha and the only one we had who could make the journey," Tex explained. "That's why we called the Alpha of the West Virginia Tigers, Jinx. He arrived moments after the team stormed the compound. Between the two of them, they might have been able to pull her through."

"But we didn't get a chance to tell her," Mason added. "She took her own life to weaken Lee, so your father could take over the clan. I know the pain is raw from the loss you suffered, but I want you to know she didn't die in vain. Jack has taken over the clan and is determined to get it back on the right track. With her actions, Lucy saved the lives of every member. The only one to die in the battle was Lee."

"Dad is the Alpha?" She leaned forward, her elbows resting on her knees as she wiped her eyes.

Mason nodded. "I can also tell you that Ethan was announced as his Lieutenant before I left and that the clan has vowed themselves to Tabitha's cause. Other than that, I'm not sure what's changed."

"Uncle Ethan will make sure her legacy lives on within the clan and more importantly, Lee can't hurt anyone anymore." Her relationship with Ethan had always been stronger than it was with her father, and as the clan's Lieutenant he'd make sure Lucy would continue to live on in the clan's memories. She blinked away the last of her tears and met Mason's gaze. "Thank you."

"I wish I could have done more." He rose from the chair and reached into his pocket. "She asked me to give you this." In his hand was the silver coin they'd made days before Lucy had been whisked away by Lee.

She leaned forward and took the coin from his outstretched hand. Bringing it close, she ran her thumb along the engravings. *LMD. Sisters by birth.* Flipping it over, she read the other side. *CMD. Best friends by choice. Always.* "We had two of these made at the mall. One for each of us." She reached into the pocket of her jeans and brought out the twin coin. "From that day forward, I carried mine with me. It's never left my possession."

"When she gave that to me, she told me it was the one thing she'd kept away from Lee, and it gave her courage to allow Jack and the others into their private quarters once Lee sent the guards away for the night." Mason took a step back and shook his head. "I feel as though I failed you."

"You didn't." Slipping out of Tex's embrace, she stood and went to him. Standing in front of him, his size dwarfed her, making her feel vulnerable.

Still, the sadness shinning in his deep blue eyes urged her forward and she timidly placed her hand on his arm. "You did everything you could for her. Just because there was a chance she could have been saved, doesn't mean that's what she wanted. She wouldn't have been the same person she was before and I don't know if she could live with the memories of what Lee did to her. She's at peace."

"From the information Jack provided, Lucy got what she wanted—a clan free of Lee's control." Tex stepped up behind her, his hand resting on her shoulder. "Jack has the same chance I had. He has to step up and be the Alpha the clan needs, to pull them back from the edge of darkness and allow them to flourish again. If he can accomplish that, then her death isn't in vain."

"If anyone can do it, Dad and Ethan can." She nodded. "He might not have been an easy man to live with and the issues between him and Mom were unbearable at times, but he always wanted what was best for the clan."

"Once things have settled, we can go see them," he assured her. "You have to give your father time to establish his rule first."

"It shouldn't be long. Jack has a firm grasp on the clan. Not like Lee had, but one that will turn the clan around," Mason added. "If you'll excuse me, I'm going to go get some sleep. If you need anything, I'll be around."

"Thank you." The grief was still raw within her, but there was also a ray of peace. Rubbing her finger along the two coins in her hand, she leaned back into Tex's body, soaking in the comfort that his touch offered.

"Oh, and…Carleen." Mason paused near the door, his hand resting on the handle. "Welcome to the team. Being an Elder has its challenges, but the rewards outweigh the negatives. When you go to Texas as the Alpha Female, remember the clan was in a worse place than the Mississippi Tigers are, and you'll be shocked at how far they've come. Tex did that, just as I believe Jack will with his clan."

"It wasn't just me."

"Modest." Mason shook his head. "While I'll agree that others have helped along the way, he's the reason for the clan's turnaround. You've got a good man there and I'm sure he'll be an excellent mate, just as he's an exceptional Alpha." With that, Mason opened the door and stepped out into the cold night air.

"He's right." She spun around to look at him. "I haven't seen it for myself yet, but I catch glimpses of the man you are whenever we touch. I can see the way Rhett follows you. His commitment to you and the clan is genuine. Robin and the others speak highly of you. Maybe that's part of why Thorn wanted to impress you so much."

"I—" She pressed her finger to his lips, cutting him off.

"Don't deny it. See what I mean? I know things I shouldn't yet. The mating isn't official and I already know you would argue with what I just said. Just as I know you doubt yourself, wondering if you're doing the right things for the clan. You need to have more confidence in yourself, in your tiger. Your beast will never steer you in the wrong direction." Chuckling lightly, she slipped the coins into the pocket of her jeans and wrapped her arms around his neck. "Maybe I should take my own advice and trust my tigress."

"Trust her with what?" His arms looped around her waist and his fingers brushed along the hem of her shirt, slipping under the material.

"That you're the right man for me." Teasing her finger along the curve of his neck, just below his cowboy hat, she smiled up at him. "I've been hesitant because you're an Alpha. Terrified I'd end up in the same situation Lucy did. But Lucy knew that Lee hadn't changed. She always knew, but I wanted to believe that love could change someone, could change him. You offered to show me more of you, to prove you're not like Lee, but if I had only listened to my tigress she'd have eliminated all my fears already."

"Sometimes our human side gets in the way of our true nature. It might take us longer to get to where we're meant to be but in the end, we find it."

"Well, I'm ready." She kept her gaze on him, watching him. Need rose within her, but she wanted him to make the first move.

"Peaches, are you sure?" His body was still under her touch, but she could feel the tight control he had on his tiger. His beast was tired of waiting.

"Yes, but not here. I don't want Thorn coming back while we're...busy. Your place?"

"I can't wait." His hands drifted lower until the grabbed her butt, lifting her up and she had no choice but to wrap her legs around his waist. "Thorn won't be back for a while. Rhett, Styx, and Felix are putting him through some additional training. We've got the place to ourselves for at least the next few hours."

"What are we waiting for? You know where the bedroom is," she teased. "Hurry."

Chapter Eleven

When Carleen was surrounded by his scent, she knew she'd found peace with Tex as her mate. Even though she hadn't realized it until that moment, she had accepted his position as Alpha and it no longer bothered her. What he'd gone through made him who he was, and that's why he was an Alpha. She couldn't fault him for what had brought them together and what would keep her safe in the future.

With every step he made toward the bedroom, her life was one step closer to a complete turnaround. She was about to go from the wallflower of the clan, always trying not to draw attention to herself, to the Alpha Female of his clan. She was terrified, but having him by her side meant she'd overcome anything the future threw at them. There was something truly special happening between them and she wasn't going to let it go. For years, she lived in fear that one day her life would end. That she would piss Lee off so much that he'd kill her. That was no longer an issue and she was ready to live life on her own terms—with Tex. She wanted the mating connection, joining them so completely that she didn't know where one of them ended and the other began. They were destined to be together, like two sides of the same coin. All she needed to do was give in to what her body craved and her tigress would do the rest.

Without pausing, he clicked the door shut behind them as he headed straight for the bed. "I need you naked." His voice was more of a growl as he lowered her onto the mattress.

"Really, now?" Shoving her nervousness aside, she leaned close to him, her fingers latching onto his belt buckle. This would be their first time. While it wouldn't be their last, she didn't want just a quick fuck. She wanted to show him how much she cared about him.

Unhooking the buckle, she kept her gaze on his face, watching as she slowly undid the leather from the metal buckle before she could reach the button and zipper of his jeans. Under the rough material, his shaft was already rock hard, straining to find freedom.

"Carleen." His tone held warning as she unhooked his jeans, but instead of freeing his shaft she pulled his shirt up. Slowly, she worked the long-sleeved shirt up his stomach, her fingers barely brushing along the contours of his chest. As she ran her hands over his pecs, he grabbed hold of the shirt and tugged it over his head.

The soft glow from the lamp on the dresser was just enough to allow her to take in the man before her. From cuddling against him earlier, she expected to find his body chiseled from working out, but what she hadn't expected was the scars that seemed to stripe his chest. For a moment, she thought they were the same mark as his tiger, that he'd been born with them, but as her fingers trailed across them she realized they were much worse.

Air escaped her lungs as she was pulled from the present, spiraling downward. She couldn't move to stop it and she found herself back in the cold, dark tunnel. This time it was a different room and there was a draft, making her shiver. As she tried to adjust to the darkness, a moan echoed off the stone walls and she forced herself forward. There before her, Tex had been strapped to a slab of stone. Blood dripped from a cut near his hairline, but it was the second man who caught her attention. Wearing fire protective gloves, he doused the rope in gasoline before lighting it on fire.

"No!" Tex hollered, but it was too late. The first slice of the rope cut through the air before landing on its target.

She reached out to him, unsure if she was reaching out to the one who was on the table before her or the one she knew stood in front of her. Fingers dug into her biceps, pulling her up and breaking her contact with his scars. The images before her began to fade, but she reached out to the man tied to the slab. Her chest tightened for the pain he was about to suffered.

"You don't need to see that." His words were enough to snap the rest of the vision like a rubber band, bringing her back to the moment.

"Oh, Tex." She stared into his eyes, unsure what to say. She wanted to touch him again, but fear of sparking another flashback kept her hands at her sides. "I'm sor—"

"Don't!" He growled, his fingers digging in a little tighter. "I don't want your sympathy."

"That's not what I meant." She reached up and pressed her hand to the side of his face, cupping his cheek in her palm. "I meant I was sorry that I brought the memories forward. You said it was our connection and you not shielding yourself from me, but I feel like I caused that."

"It's both of us." He let go of her arms and pulled his cowboy hat off, quickly tossing it on the nightstand, next to the picture of her family. "As you touched the rough, hideous scars, it shattered the shields I had in place."

"Why?" He was silent for long enough that she wasn't sure he'd answer her.

"You're the first person who has ever touched them. The simple caress was my undoing. You touched them as if they weren't as hideous as I know they are. As if they didn't matter to you."

"They don't." She slid her hand down his cheek, slowly working her way back to the scars. They both had enough control over themselves that she didn't slip back into the vision. As the tips of her fingers made contact with the edge of the first scar, his muscles tightened and he started to pull away from her. Hooking her finger in the belt loop of his jeans, she kept him close as her other hand continued to explore the contours of each horrible wound. She didn't have to look at each of the lashes to know he'd received ten different ones. Three of them intersected, making them appear larger than the others.

"They're part of you and how you received them is horrible, but they're not hideous." Staring into his eyes, she waited for his body to relax. "Focus on me and you'll know that I'm not disgusted by these. They change nothing."

"I felt your sympathy."

"That you had to suffer through that torment, not because there are scars." Her chest tightened as she remembered the fierce pain of the rope lashing his skin and the flames burning his stomach. It was as if she'd suffered through it, but she only witnessed it through his memory. "The pain I felt in that brief scene was nothing like what you went through. I know they kept you tied to that slab with a collar on, to keep you from shifting. Even after the infection set in, you were left there to deal with the pain until the wounds healed. That's why you felt my empathy."

Unsure what to do and not wanting to push him, she waited for him to say something but he remained quiet. With a deep breath, she decided it was time to go all in. Taking hold of the hem of her shirt, she slowly pulled it up and over her head. "Don't push me away, Tex. Nothing has changed. I want you. All of you."

"Are you sure about this? Before this mating is cemented, you're going to see more…"

"Just as you're going to see things about me. That's how mating works. There are no secrets between mates. By the time we're through, I'll know everything there is to know about you, just as you will with me." She pressed her lips to his, kissing him softly before drawing his bottom lip between her teeth and nipping lightly before letting go again. "Our past doesn't matter. It's our future *together* that does."

"So wise and beautiful. No wonder you're my perfect match." He tangled his fingers in her hair. "I came here to pick out guards, but if it wasn't for Rhett that would have been a neglected task. I can't get you out of my thoughts. My tiger demands to be near you and when I'm not, he's on edge, ready to fight anyone who makes the wrong move."

"Soon that connection will be cemented and even when we're not in the same room, we'll be connected, putting your tiger at ease." She eased the waistband of his jeans down, letting them fall. "You're an Alpha, you want to protect those around you, especially your mate and without that connection your beast is worried he'll fail."

"Something could happen and I wouldn't have known you were in danger."

"No." She shook her head. "This connection between us is stronger than that. You'd have known, but it doesn't matter now. Claim me."

His arms wrapped around her body as his mouth claimed her lips as his fingers unhooked her bra. Not satisfied with the sweet kiss, she wanted more, so she slipped her tongue into his mouth. She wanted him more than anything else and to prove that, she tugged at the waistband of his boxers, easing them downward and wrapping her hand around his shaft.

She rubbed down the length, painstakingly slow, applying just enough pressure that he arched toward her. She loved the soft moan escaping his lips. "Tex, please…I need you," she whispered.

He pulled gently away, forcing her to let go of him, and stripped her bra from her. "Take off your jeans and lie back on the bed."

Doing what he asked, she stripped out of her remaining clothes, including her panties, and crawled onto the bed to recline on the pillows. "Are you going to join me?"

His clothes were off and he was crouched on top of her in a blink of an eye. He pressed his lips to hers with such desire that she moaned around his unrelenting kiss. Reaching for his biceps, she tried to bring him closer, but he kept his arms straight, refusing to give in. When the kiss ended, leaving her breathless, he stayed arched above her. "Beautiful. The ruby red waves of your hair, spilling around your shoulders brings out the warm golden hues of your amber eyes. Your pale skin with these adorable freckles make me want to run my tongue over every inch of you, connecting the dots."

He nipped and licked along her skin, working his way toward her breast, gently purring. His body vibrated against hers, keeping her on edge until his mouth locked feverishly around her nipple. As his tongue flicked over the hardened bud, her last shred of patience slipped away. She needed him and she couldn't wait any longer. She reached out, placing her hand firmly on his chest, her desire escalating. His shaft pressed tight against her thigh, pulsing with his own need, and she arched her body into him.

"Please—" All words were stolen from her as he slipped his fingers between her legs, sliding over her clit, pulling the pleasure from her inch by inch. He thrust his fingers into her as his thumb continued to pull more pleasure from her core.

She couldn't stop herself from touching him. She reached out and caressed the arch of his hips, teasing along the curve and up his sides. Desire poured through her as she wiggled against him, needing his touch, wanting more than his finger. She wanted him inside of her. "I need you. Please…"

"Peaches." He sucked her earlobe into his mouth, his teeth grazing around her earring, his hand sliding down her body, following her curves.

"What do you need?"

"I need you."

"You have me." His thumb teased over her clit at a new angle, causing her body to jerk against his.

"Inside me. Please, Tex, inside me!" Her voice rose and she could only hope that no one outside could hear her. Practically panting, she arched toward him. Desperation flooded through her. "Now…" The mating desire rolled within her, unwilling to be denied. Her tigress was anxious to have her mate. She needed him inside of her and she wanted it now.

"Didn't anyone teach you that an Alpha doesn't take orders?" His lips circled her nipple, grazing his teeth over it until she arched into him.

"Don't consider it an order…I'm begging," she moaned as his hand slid away from her pussy.

He tore his lips away from her breast, leaning up to look at her. "Your tigress has been vibrating along the surface, urging me on, but when I pulled back I could feel her snarling at me. Baby, do you really think I'd deny you what you need?" Watching her, he waited for an answer.

"You want it as bad as I do. I…we need this." Her fingers wrapped around his bicep to stop herself from clawing down his body.

Slipping between her legs, he positioned himself just above her pussy. "Are you sure you're ready?"

"Yes!" The answer was filled with need.

"An orgasm will tear down all the walls between us, so you need to brace yourself for what you'll see and the flood of emotions you'll feel from the clan as you accept your position as Alpha Female."

Forcing herself to open her eyes, she looked up at him and the anxiety that reflected in his gaze tightened her chest. "Baby, you're worrying for nothing. I'm ready. Nothing is going to change this. This is our destiny." She reached up and dragged her finger along the curve of his cheek. "We'll handle it and everything else that life throws at us, together."

"When it starts, just remember it will be over quickly. I'll be there with you and I'll never break contact." He leaned down to her and pressed his lips to hers in a soft kiss. "Mate, in the few days I've know you, I've fallen in love with you. The emotions you spark within me are ones I thought were long dead. I never thought I'd have someone in my life who means what you mean to me. I love you already and the future will be brighter just having you by my side. You're mine as I'm yours." Before she could reply, he kissed her again, this time deeper, more passionately, stealing the breath from her.

He pulled his mouth from hers and kissed a path down her neck. His breath was cool against her skin, sending goosebumps down her body as he nipped and kissed along her shoulder. She had wanted to say she looked forward to that, but the words were stuck in her throat as she fought to keep the screams of desire from springing forward. Sensations collided and threatened to overwhelm her, but she pushed her beast away, trying to savor the moment.

"You're mine. I'll protect and cherish you until my dying day." He kissed down her chest until he reached her breasts, dragging his tongue in lazy circles around her nipples. The intensity of her desire shot through every cell of her body. Teasing her nipples gently, pulling them between his teeth until they stood at attention, he rested his weight on an elbow and used the other hand to explore the length of her body. His fingers teased along every curve until it felt like fire sparked between them, growing stronger and hotter with each touch.

Her mind was in a sexual haze, and her beast was just below the surface, speeding the pace, clawing at her insides, demanding to be set free to mingle with his. Words wouldn't come to her but as her hands roamed along his body, she hoped he could sense what she was feeling for him. The love she already had for him was something she knew would grow as they got to know each other better.

Lifting her hips off the bed, he spread her legs farther, giving him the access he needed. Their gazes met for a moment as she watched the battle within his eyes. His beast clashed against his control, fighting to be set free. The foreplay had snapped his tiger's tolerance and he needed to claim her. He tried to draw it out, giving her everything he thought she needed, when what she craved most was him inside of her.

"Baby…now." In that moment, all that mattered was joining the two of them together in a bond stronger than anything else on this planet. She needed her mate, her Alpha. He was the piece within her that had been missing and now she could be whole.

Without waiting a moment longer, he slid his shaft into her warm, wet core, his manhood filling her completely. Her tigress leapt forward to meet him. With every thrust, his pace sped and their beasts mingled together like an invisible blanket surrounding them. Stroke after stroke, the tempo between them intensified until his hips where slamming off hers, a driving force with each pump. The thrusts became deeper and faster, falling into a perfect rhythm. Their bodies rocked back and forth and she arched into him, holding onto his lower back to bring them closer together. The tension strained through their muscles as she fought for the release she longed for.

She stared up at him, lost in his eyes. They were no longer the normal storm gray, but had turned the bright yellow of his tiger. Still within them, she could see the slivers of gray that reminded her of lightning. The power she saw drew her in as she clung to him. "Tex."

"It's okay, sweetie." His voice was barely more than a growl. "Yours are, too."

She tipped her head to the side to look into the mirror above the dresser. In the reflection, her tiger's eyes shined back but that wasn't what caught her attention; it was Tex's body as he pumped into her. An image popped into her head, but before she could focus on it, Tex nipped at her neck, bringing her back to the moment.

"You'll give a man a complex if you keep staring in that mirror."

"I love watching you fuck me." Growing more excited, she arched up to meet him. Faster and deeper, they met each other's thrusts. They climbed the mountain, both seeking the apex. Their moans mixed with purrs and growls as the tsunami of ecstasy flooded toward her.

"Tex!" Screaming his name, she arched her body into his as her release coursed through her, her nails digging into his shoulders and leaving angry red scratches. He continued to pump into her, his tempo never missing a beat as the waves tore through her. With one final push, he drove into her, tipped his head back and roared as his release followed.

She sank back onto the pillows as the flood of memories and emotions hit her. Every aspect of his life flashed before her closed eyes and she shuddered at the horrors she saw. She reached for him, but he was no longer on top of her.

"I'm here, sweetie." Unable to open her eyes, she felt him roll her toward him, cuddling her against his body.

She clung to him, reminding herself that everything she'd witnessed made him the man he was. The tortures he suffered at the hands of Avery were over. Avery was dead and Tex was alive. Nothing would change that. Knowing the horrors he'd suffered through would never happened to anyone else did little to ease the knot in her chest, because he still had to live with the memories and the scars. Her mate had survived, but how many others had died because of his tormenter?

Chapter Twelve

Watching the horrors of his past had very little effect on Tex. He lived through it, so nothing he saw was a surprise, but watching Carleen squeeze her eyes shut and cling to him as it flashed before her tore at his soul. He wanted to stop it from happening but there was nothing he could do. All mates went through this to some degree. With Elders, it was more complete. Elder mates needed to know everything about each other so nothing could ever be used against them. Some might experience it in smaller doses. Unfortunately for Carleen, the bond between them was too strong and he'd already pulled her into his flashbacks. Now she was forced to witness his life unfold before her very eyes.

"No…" A moan tore through her and her body shook violently against his.

He cuddled her against his body, holding her tight enough that she knew she wasn't alone. All he could do was wait for it to pass. "Peaches, I'm here. You're not there. Focus on my voice."

Her fingers dug into his chest, digging deep enough that blood seeped from the grooves. Rubbing his hand along her back, he stayed focused on her, doing what little he could to comfort her. Pressing his lips to the top of her head, he took in her scent, letting her sweet aroma of fresh peaches keep his attention so he wouldn't focus on the torture that was playing out before them right now. The pain of the scalding oil as it landed on his arms was something he couldn't deny. It happened in the past, but he could feel it now as if it was happening again.

"We're almost done." He rolled toward her, pressing the front of their bodies together, intertwining their legs and wrapping both arms around her. Resting his head on the pillow above her, he kept his face pressed against the top of her head. His lips brushed along her hairline, planting soft kisses there.

"No!" She tried to pull away, but he held her tight. "Please…you can't…die…"

"Shh, Carleen. It's going to be fine." His eyelids drifted shut and he could see himself lying on the same stone slab he was on when Avery whipped him with the burning rope. Only this time there were burns up and down his arms and legs from where Avery had splashed hot oil before finally slicing his throat. As he choked on his own blood and fear filled his eyes, he realized Avery was smirking. Everyone from the clan knew Avery got off on the torture, but until that moment Tex hadn't realized what an impact it had on his former Alpha.

At the time, he had been so wrapped up in his own thoughts that he hadn't looked at Avery. While lying there and bleeding out, he thought the end was finally coming. A mixture of emotions poured through him, the strongest being sadness that there was so much he hadn't done and relief knowing that Avery's torture was over, at least for him. When he was finally unstrapped from the slab, he almost allowed himself the pleasure of slipping away.

Don't you die on me. I need you. Autumn and Summer need you. Damn it, we all need you. Ben's words echoed through the room, reminding him of the reason he forced himself to shift and heal. He wanted to give in to the blood loss and the pain and allow it to carry him off to his death, but there were people counting on him. People he couldn't leave behind. Ben was his best friend and partner on guard duty. They needed each other to survive.

"Tex." She called his name as he was shoved into one of the small rooms in the tunnel. Alone in that room, he spent weeks without any human contact, driving him nearly insane. "Tex?"

"I'm here." Placing his hand on the side of her face, he wiped away the tear before it could roll down her cheek. "Don't cry."

"I'm so sorry that happened to you." Wrapping her arm around his back, she clung to him.

"It brought me to you and that's what matters." He leaned back to look at her. "It's not over yet."

"The worst is." She opened her eyes to meet his gaze. "Watching everything play out in front of me and not being able to do anything to help you was torture. My past might not be sunshine and roses, but it's not like what you went through. It won't faze you."

Before he was able to reply, the second part of the mating connection flooded toward them. Even though it wasn't as overpowering as the first, he was thankful for that moment of reprieve, allowing him to comfort her.

Moments later, the rest of the mating ritual was over and they were connected on every level. Each of their pasts had been witnessed and there were no secrets between them. She remained cuddled against him, holding him tight. On one level, that surprised him. After everything she'd witnessed, she still wanted to be there with him and none of it had changed how she perceived him. When he looked back at his past, he cursed himself for being weak. He should have done something, fought back against his former Alpha long before he stood with Ty and the others as they brought Avery down.

"You protected the others and that took courage." She ran her hand up his chest. "The tortures you endured proved you're not weak."

"I was too afraid to stand up to him. That's weakness."

"No, Tex, that's self-preservation. If you'd have gotten yourself killed, the torture your clan went through would still be happening. You not only protected them when you could, you saved them when you had the opportunity. That's why they follow you now."

Unsure what to say, he caressed her side with his fingers, moving in lazy strokes. The doubts and regrets within him that he kept concealed from everyone else could no longer be hidden from her. Their connection opened her to that part of him even if he wanted to keep it hidden. He wanted to protect her from anything that could harm her, but there was no protection from that side of him.

"I guess I should be thankful you're not arguing with me." She cocked her head up from where it rested on his arm and looked up at him.

"A smart man knows better than to argue with his mate." He shot her a halfhearted grin.

"I wish it was because you realized I'm right, but I'll take that at least. In time, I'll prove it to you." Sliding her hand between their bodies and down his chest she eased lower until she was brushing against his manhood.

"What are you doing?"

"Isn't it obvious?" As her fingers wrapped around him, his shaft responded, growing hard under her touch. "Tomorrow you're leaving for Texas, so we need to make the most of this time."

"You're coming with me." He arched his hips toward her. "My mate goes where I go."

"I never said I wasn't." Teasingly, she dragged her hand up and down his length. "I should have said *we're* leaving for Texas. But the point is still the same. The members know you're here recruiting but some are leery of adding new people to the clan, especially new guards in a position of power. You're going to be busy and before you correct me, you should realize that they'll be suspicious of me, too. Your mate or not, I'm an outsider. I'm going to have to prove myself to them and I will, but it won't happen overnight. Too much of this transition is going to fall on you. I'll help where I can, but I don't want to push them."

"You're underestimating them. They're going to love you. But you're right, we're going to be busy, so there's no reason why we can't take a little more time for ourselves now." He leaned into her, his lips brushing against hers. "I'm going to make love to you, then we're going to pack your stuff up for tomorrow and you're coming back to my cabin. I'm not sure if sleep is on the agenda, but I want you with me and if I want to make you purr my name again, I don't want Thorn listening."

"Having Rhett listening is so much better." She rolled her eyes. "I think you're going to be stuck waiting until we're back in Texas."

"I'll kick him out." He rolled her onto her back and hovered above her. "He can stay here with Thorn. Hell, I don't care where he stays as long as we're alone together."

Kissing along her collarbone, he worked his way up her neck as her fingers trailed along the sides of his chest. "I like the sound of that."

"Me too, sweetie." His cell phone rang, making him dip his head in defeat. "Shit."

"Get it. I understand."

"No, you don't." He reached over the side of the bed and snatched his jeans off the floorboard. As he pulled the cell phone out of his pocket, he caught sight of the number, recognizing it immediately. He cursed his luck. Just as he expected. "You didn't have a secure cell phone, so I told Mason to give him this number."

"Who?"

"Your father." He held the phone out to her. "I knew you'd want to talk to him, so Mason gave him this number and told him to call you when he had things under control. Jack has his hands full and unless we wanted to make things more complicated for him, it was best to leave the ball in his court. Plus, I didn't want you getting hurt."

"I don't know what to say to him."

"You both lost someone you loved. You're feeling guilty because you encouraged Lucy to accept the mating, but imagine what Jack is going through. Lucy took her own life to save his. The guilt he's carrying will be with him for the rest of his life. The two of you need each other now. You can ease each other's pain, but more than that, you're his only living daughter. He'll want to reestablish that connection with you." He pressed the phone into her hand. "Talk to him. The words will come when you need them and I'll be here."

Putting off the call with her father would only make Carleen more apprehensive of the whole conversation. Even though she wasn't in Mississippi, she still felt guilty about what had happened. How bad had things gotten once she and Thorn left? What torment had Lee put Lucy and her father through because they'd abandoned the clan? Accepting the call might give her answers she wasn't sure she was ready for. Dragging her bottom lip between her teeth, she pressed a button and brought the phone to her ear. "Dad?"

"Zoom, it's so good to hear your voice." There was a heaviness in his tone that she'd never heard before. She couldn't remember a time where he showed any sign of emotion other than anger.

"You too, Dad. I've missed you." She leaned back on the pillows and let her eyelids close to hide the tears welling in her eyes.

Until that moment, she hadn't realized how much she missed her father.

Their relationship had been rough for so many years, but when her mother passed away he seemed to become a different man. They formed a bond and she clung to the new relationship because she knew their time together would be short. One day she'd mate, and he hoped the mating would force her to leave the clan, giving her a freedom she didn't have there. Against both of their wishes the bond grew stronger, bringing them closer than she was with Uncle Ethan.

"When Mason gave me the number, he didn't tell me much except this was the Alpha of the Texas Tiger's cell phone and the best way to reach you. Last I heard from my contact, you and Thorn were in Alaska. Imagine my surprise to learn you're in Texas. Is Thorn with you? Have you committed to this Alpha?" Concern laced his voice as the questions rushed at her. She wondered if he was concerned their conversation might be cut short, or that she could be in danger.

"Everything's fine." Without opening her eyes, she reached forward, quickly finding Tex's hand. "We're still in Alaska, but tomorrow we're going to Texas."

"Are you sure about that? You can come home. It's safe now."

"I'll come visit." Opening her eyes, she found Tex nodding. "Thorn will come with me, too. But we can't come back…well, I can't."

"What do you mean, you can't? Zoom, are you in some kind of trouble? Is someone forcing you to go to Texas?"

"Tell him," Tex urged.

"Who's that?" her father demanded before she could say anything. "Answer me. Who's there with you?"

"Everything is fine. The Alpha of the Texas Tigers, Tex, is here. He's…umm…" Her breath caught in her throat. "My mate."

"Oh, Carleen." A roar resonated through the phone, quickly followed by a loud bang as if something had crashed to the floor.

"Dad, it's not like that. Tex is a good man. You'd approve of him."

"Where's Thorn? I want to speak with him."

"He's not here now, but I can have him call you later. Thorn is going through another training session before we leave tomorrow. Tex wants to make sure he's ready for his new role." She didn't expand on Thorn's new position mostly because Thorn didn't even know Tex planned to have him as the Captain of her Guards. If her brother decided not to accept the position, she wasn't even sure he'd stay. For all she knew, he'd end up going back to Mississippi. He could be a great ally to their father, but for her own selfish reasons she wanted him with her. He had always watched out for her and the idea of going to Texas without him was unnerving.

"He's supposed to be keeping you safe."

"He has. Trust me, he wasn't happy about this mating either, but it's my destiny—"

"We saw what destiny had in store for Lucy. Shit, Zoom, I wanted better for you."

"Even if you had the opportunity to hand-select my mate from all the men on the planet, I don't think you could have picked anyone better for me." She squeezed Tex's hand. Not out of sympathy but to remind him of their solidarity. They were in this together and she wouldn't change it. "We'll visit soon and you'll see. This is different from Lucy's mating."

"I don't want to see you miserable like she was."

"This is different." Not knowing how to convince him of that, she stated the same thing again as she interlaced her fingers with Tex's. "Lucy knew Lee wasn't different, but I wouldn't listen to her. Maybe if I kept my mouth shut, she wouldn't have lived through torment the last few years. Dad, she's finally free. Please take my word for it. Tex isn't like Lee."

"You can't be sure. Lucy wasn't."

"She was. She just hid it from all of us until it was too late. She didn't want us to know. She was scared of what you and Thorn would do." Her sister had always been more concerned about everyone else around her. Even after Lee claimed her, she tried to protect them from what was happening behind closed doors, except she couldn't hide the bruises or her shaved head.

"I should have killed Lee years ago," he snapped. "She'd still be alive if I'd done it when I should have."

"You don't know that. None of us know what life would be like if we'd taken a different split in the road. We don't get to go back and make a change to the path we've chosen. All we can do is make the best of the choices we've made." In her mind, she could see her father standing there in their small house, surrounded by all the memories of the life they lived. For the first time, it dawned on her that he was alone. She needed to talk to Thorn and find out what he wanted to do. Maybe instead of going to Texas, he wanted to return home. It would change Tex's plan for her protection, but then her father would have help. Tex could promote someone else as the Captain of her Guards.

"The choices we think are right at the time often turn out to be the ones that cost us the most." He let out a deep breath, groaning. "After I ordered Thorn to get you out of there, Lucy had a spark in her eye that I hadn't seen in years. She was happy knowing you were somewhere safe and out of Lee's reach. When she came to me about eliminating Lee, we went over the possibilities. We knew the risks we were taking and I realized I might lose her, but it's what she wanted. She wanted to be free from him, even if that meant only in death."

"I think she always knew her only way of escaping Lee was through death. She's at peace and the clan is free. That's what she wanted."

"You don't understand. I failed her." The pain in his voice had her fingers tightening around the comforter. The guilt would plague him for the rest of his life, just as her own did.

"I know what happened." Mason's words flooded back to her, painting the picture before her eyes again. "She did what she had to. She saved your life, and she saved everyone. Dad, you didn't fail anyone. Lee was cheating and she knew what it would mean if he survived. I have no doubt she was prepared to die from the moment she opened the door for you. If she could have survived Lee's death, facing life without her mate would have been one thing but continuing without you and knowing what torture awaited her...she couldn't face that. You were the clan's one shot and she wasn't going to allow that to pass them by."

"Someone stronger should have taken it then. Someone younger," her father snapped.

"You were the clan's best shot at defeating him and you know it. This isn't about your age or strength. Lee was cheating," she reminded him again. "What matters now if that you turn the clan into what Lucy wanted. Turn things around and don't let her death be a waste. Make sure she lives on within the clan."

"Jack, we're ready," a deep voice called, but she couldn't make out who it was.

"Zoom, Ethan's here. I need to go. We're meeting to get our guard rotations up and running."

"Give Uncle Ethan my love. I'm proud of you both. I know you two can turn the clan back into something amazing." Part of her wished she could be there to see the changes, but she was happy with what was happening between her and Tex.

Within twenty-four hours, they'd be in Texas and she'd have her work cut out for her as she got the clan to accept her as Alpha Female. The near future would hold a visit to Mississippi, but until then, they both had things requiring their attention. In a couple of months, she was sure her father would have the clan on the path to success just as Tex had done with the Texas Tigers.

Chapter Thirteen

After the phone call ended, Tex slipped into bed. Lying next to Carleen, he wrapped his arms around her. Her emotions were bouncing from sorrow, to relief, to joy, and instead of pressing her he waited. She'd confide in him when she was ready. Until then, he was content having her body cuddled against his.

"Thank you." She tipped her head up from his chest. "For knowing I needed to talk to him and for encouraging me to take the call. He needed to hear from me as much as I needed it."

"Even before we were mated, the relationship you have with Jack vibrated along the edge of our connection. I don't want to come between that, but you need to realize it's going to take time before you can go to Mississippi." He watched her for a moment, expecting her to question him. Instead, she remained quiet. "From what Mason told me, I don't except an uproar from the members. They all seem relieved to be rid of Lee. My concern is with outsiders seeing the clan as an easy target. We need to give it a few weeks before visiting. It will allow Jack to stand on his own paws and show others he's not weak. That will eliminate a lot of the threat to them and it will also mean it's safe for you."

"What if he needs help?"

"Then we'll help. He's not alone, but his rule must be his own. Other clans can't come to his aid to ward off those who challenge his position. He'll have to do that himself. If there's a threat to the clan, we can help. Ty and

Tabitha aren't going to allow an ally clan to be attacked and slaughtered." He pressed his lips to her forehead. "You should already know I would send whoever I can to help Jack if he needs it. He's family."

"You say family as if you know what it's like, but the only similar connection you have is the one with Ben. Before he became your Lieutenant, he was your closest friend, an ally. Some shifters don't have family connections out of choice, but yours wasn't by choice."

"The clan is my family. It's all I've known."

"What about the tigress who raised you?" Teasing her finger down his abs before slowly working her way back, she watched him.

"She was a good woman and I'll always be thankful for her taking me in, but she wasn't family. There was a wall between us, dividing any bond I might have wanted. She did it to protect herself because Avery had his eye on me. Developing too much of a link would have given Avery something else to hold over us. Instead, she kept me at arm's length and that distance only grew when I was a teenager and he had me working as a guard."

"She cared enough to make sure you received the education Avery tried to deprive you of."

"Out of duty." He dragged his hand through her hair, watching the silky strands slide through his fingers. "That's not fair to her. She did it so I had a chance. If I had the education she could give me and the training as a guard, I had a chance. Without it, what did I have to offer an Elder or even my mate?"

"You have a lot to offer." She snuggled closer, draping her leg over his. "I don't know what kind of person you'd have been without her kindness. Maybe you'd have been harder or filled with hatred. I witnessed the torment you went through and all that shit made you stronger. I love having you as my mate and I'm looking forward to our future together."

"What a change in a matter of days." He let out a light chuckle, vibrating his chest.

"I know I wasn't as welcoming to the idea of having an Alpha as a mate, but you surprised me. I was scared of what being mated to an Alpha meant. I didn't want to have the same horrible relationship my parents had or be stuck in a situation like Lucy was."

"I don't think you have to worry about that," he teased. "That is unless you're hiding some hatred for me. So, tell me, why does he call you Zoom?"

"Zoom." A smile curled up the corners of her lips. "Lucy was close with Mom, making me feel left out. All our lives, Thorn and I were close but he also had his own thing. Dad was alone, so I tried to have that same relationship with him. Our relationship was rocky most of my life, but there were moments when they were wonderful. One of those special times is when the nickname started and kind of stuck. No one ever asked about it and unless Dad told someone else, it was just between us."

"Go on," he encouraged.

"Dad worked construction most of my life and until Lee stopped allowing people to leave for work every day, he owned his own business. It was a small company, but he was proud of it. Sometimes he'd allow me to tag along with him when he was going to check on projects his crew was assigned to. That day he had his crews spread out on a couple projects, so it was going to be a long day driving from one job site to another. I still wanted to go. It was a break from the clan and a few hours of freedom. I don't remember what he yelled at me for, but to make up for it he pulled me into his lap and let me drive." Grinning ear to ear, she chuckled.

"How old were you?"

"Seven, I think. It was just a dirt road leading back to a new housing development, so there wasn't any oncoming traffic or anything. Now I realize he had his hand resting gently on the bottom of the wheel, making sure we stayed on the road, but at that time I thought I was doing it myself. It felt amazing. The sensation of freedom was overwhelming. I wanted to just drive away and forget about all the crap that was starting within the clan. He seemed so happy and I didn't want to go back. The man he was when we were out checking on the job sites was so different from the one I lived with." She tugged the blanket up over her shoulder and returned her hand to his chest. "While I was pretending to drive, I kept making these zooming noises. He teased me about it and I guess the nickname just kind of stuck."

"Memories like that are what allowed you to build a relationship with him. They helped you let go of the hatred you witnessed between him and your mother. As the clan remembers their own moments like that, they'll find it easier to put Lee's torment behind them and rebuild their lives." He squeezed her a little tighter against his side. "Now, as much as I'd love to stay cuddled in here with your naked body pressed against me, I think we should get up."

"Why?" She snuggled against him, working the blanket farther up toward her chin. "The bed is so warm and outside...well, you know what it is. It's Alaska, freezing and snowy. Let's just stay here and kick Thorn out."

"Sorry, peaches, but my cabin is set up for visiting Elders. There's a communication device in the bedroom so I know what's happening. In the unlikeliness that the cabin was breached, there's even a secret escape. It's a precaution, but that's where we need to be tonight." He pulled back the covers, revealing her naked body and all thoughts of getting out of bed nearly vanished. "But that's not why I suggested we get up."

"Then why did you?" She shivered against him and her nipples hardened, making him want to roll her over and suck them into his mouth.

"You should know, you're connected to the clan now. Focus on Rhett."

He forced himself to move to the edge of the bed and gather his clothes. Before any of them could sleep, he needed a few minutes with Thorn to discuss the guard position and he wanted to be dressed for that conversation. Thorn wanted to protect his sister, and he was starting to accept Carleen and Tex being mates. Still, the last thing he needed was to find them naked in bed together.

"Oh shit!" She hopped out of bed. "I wasn't paying attention and I barely noticed Rhett's emotions. I didn't even realize they were on their way back."

"You still have a lot going on to keep your thoughts entertained, and it's not surprising you have strong walls within your mind to keep the clan from overwhelming you. Tomorrow will be the test to see if they can withstand it." He tugged on his jeans. "Unless you want your brother to know how we've spent the time together, you might want to get dressed."

"Spent the time? You mean packing and talking to Dad? You know, somehow I don't think he'll be upset about that." She shot him a cocky smile as she tugged on her jeans.

"Smart ass." He tugged his shirt over his head. "I'm going to grab a cup of coffee. Want one?"

Buttoning her jeans, she shook her head. "You're going to want me to skip the caffeine and get eight hours of sleep if I'm going to be cheerful tomorrow when I meet your clan. Trust me when I say my claws come out when I'm tired."

"I can't remember the last time I got eight hours of uninterrupted sleep." Shaking his head, he strolled toward the door. "Being an Elder plays hell on your sleep schedule."

"Keep it up with those helpful tidbits and I might decide killing you is a better option than being mated to you." Slipping her sweater over her head, she followed him toward the kitchen.

"Believe what you want." He leaned against the wall closer to the living room and as she neared, he wrapped his arms around her, drawing her against his body. "You know you'd miss what we have. The way your body fits against mine because you're meant to be there. You're mine and while there might be times when you're sleep deprived, I'll make up for it in other ways."

"What ways?" Before he could answer, the front door opened and Thorn ambled into the cabin, Rhett close behind.

"I see you're packed." Thorn nodded to the suitcases by the door. "I figured you'd have already left."

"She's going to come stay with me, but we wanted to talk to you. Let me grab a cup of coffee first. Anyone else want a cup?" Without waiting for an answer, Tex strolled toward the kitchen.

"It's late and unless you have more tests to put me through, I'll pass." Thorn dropped down onto the chair in the living room. Exhaustion rolled off him but his eyes were alert, giving him a bump up in Tex's opinion. "Well…"

"Well what?" Tex glanced toward the living room, the coffee pot in his hand.

"Dawson and Brody both know they've got a position in Texas and neither of them had to go through these additional tests. So, what's up? Did I secure a spot or not?"

With his coffee in hand, Tex moved to the end of the counter where Carleen was lingering out of the way and slipped his arm around her waist, drawing her against him. Letting Thorn's uneasiness grow, he took a drink of his coffee before lifting his gaze away from his mate and focusing on her brother. "I came here looking for guards to ensure the safety of my clan.

With the resort opening soon, the threat level goes up. I need to ensure not only the clan and guests are safe, but that we're ready for any situation that arrives. Which means I need to find a couple of strong guards to help train more until our team is running at full capacity. I'm open to recruiting from other clans, but until some construction is complete, it limits how many recruits I can bring onboard. So, I need the strongest and the best warriors available to me."

"I understand. I appreciate the opportunity." Thorn slammed his hands on his thighs and started to rise. "Car, we need to talk. *Privately.*"

"Sit down. We're not done." Tex watched him with annoyance as he waited for him to sit back down. "From the moment you found me and Carleen in the kitchen, your attitude has been working under my skin. I realize you're stressed, but giving your anger an outlet is going to cost you dearly."

"My attitude is the reason you're not giving me a position?" Thorn's gaze shifted from Tex to Carleen, then back to Tex. "I was trying to protect my sister. After what your clan went through and the news of Lucy's death, I would have thought you'd understand. I guess compassion isn't something Alphas comprehend."

"Thorn!" Carleen scolded.

"No, Carleen." Thorn's fingers tightened around the arm of the chair as he continued to stare at them. "The person he's seen is the real me. There's nothing I wouldn't do to protect you. You're my little sister and we've always been close. I can't stand by as some new Alpha comes in and the past repeats itself. Don't expect me to do nothing. I won't allow you to end up the same way Lucy did."

"It's not the—"

"That's what I mean." The fabric of the chair ripped as Thorn dug his fingers in deeper. "You're always so quick to defend him. Even before he claimed you. You've always wanted to believe in fairytales and a happily-ever-after, but that's not real life. Look at Lee. You wanted to believe he'd changed but if anything, he got worse."

"That attack is exactly why I shouldn't offer you a guard position." He held her tighter to him, trying to ease her tension with his touch so they could get the conversation over with. "Your blatant disregard for authority and your sister's feelings is more than enough to remove you from the running, and depending on Ty's decision eliminate you from future possible guard positions."

"The first might be your decision, but the second one isn't. At the very least I should have an opportunity to present my side to Ty before he removes me from the program." Thorn shifted uneasily in his seat. "Maybe Raja can understand my position. He'd do the same if it was Tora's safety at risk."

"Unlike what I've witnessed from you, Raja knows what battles to fight and when to keep his mouth shut. Good thing for you I truly believe you're irritated because you're afraid for Carleen's life and that's the only reason you've lasted this long. Otherwise, I'd have already eliminated you." He took another sip from his coffee mug. "Carleen means a great deal to you, to both of us. As my mate, she's in danger not only for my support of Tabitha, but also from those who supported Avery. While they might no longer be part of the clan, they're still a threat. With the resort opening, no amount of background checks or security in place will eliminate the danger surrounding her and that has helped to keep you in the running."

"What? I don't understand what you're talking about."

"I want you in Texas with us. As—" Unease rushed through him and he looked at Carleen just as she turned toward him and slipped her arms around his waist. She was afraid her brother would reject the position and that fear was nearly overwhelming. He opened the connection between them, allowing her to hear him. *It's okay, peaches.*

"As what?" Thorn pressed.

"The Captain of Carleen's Guards." With his focus on her brother, he rubbed his hand down her back. "If you want the position, you're going to need to change your attitude."

"Why offer me the position?"

"I'm aware of the conversation you've had with her and that you're willing to challenge me if it will keep her safe. You might not believe this, but I understand where you're coming from. You want her safe." He glanced down at her. "That's what I want, too."

"What if the threat to her safety is you?" Thorn's voice remained steady, though something shifted in his eyes.

"Soon enough you'll realize that there's nothing more important to me than her happiness and safety." With one last sip, he set the coffee aside and teased his hand up her arm. "If you find proof that I'm an Alpha who's anything like Lee, then challenge me."

"If I lost, she'd be at your mercy." He caught the change in Thorn's voice. The fight was gone, but he continued because he couldn't trust himself enough to know Tex was different. It was clear in his voice, his posture, and most of all his scent.

"Ty and Tabitha would never allow me to continue as Alpha if I was turning into someone like Avery or Lee. The clan has been through too much and we're just putting the pieces of our lives back together. I'm committed to Ty and Tabitha. As the King and Queen of the tigers, they can feel the Alpha I am. They know how I run my clan and my true beliefs. If there was ever a hint that I'd become a vindictive Alpha, they'd swoop in and rescue the clan before damage could be done."

"Fear of the unknown is what has you holding on to this insane idea." She stepped out of his embrace and moved toward her brother. "We both know if Tex wasn't an Elder, you'd look at him differently. You'd respect him for what he's accomplished and what he's overcome. Those same reasons are why you should be honored to serve under him. A young Alpha who's brought his clan back from ashes and is building something amazing in Texas. Manetka Resort is going to be back, better than ever. I want to be part of that and I want you to be, too, but I understand if you can't."

"If I can't."

"Yeah, Thorn. If you can't let go of your anger and learn to respect Tex, then what else is there for you to do but find a different clan."

Her sorrow stabbed Tex in the stomach. He knew she wanted Thorn in Texas, but he hadn't realized how much her brother's decision weighed on her. She wasn't just anxious he would reject the position, she was scared she'd lose him. Whether he went back to Mississippi or found another clan, the loss would be the same. Rather than going to her like his tiger demanded, he hung back and gave her the opportunity to let her brother know how she felt.

"I want you safe, Car." Thorn's shoulder relaxed. "Every time I think of you being mated to an Alpha I think about the hell Lucy went through and how we were all helpless to stop it. Lee's supporters were very few, but most of us were too scared to do something. Lee made sure he had someone to hold over the clan's head if they tried anything. Dad kept his people in line for Lucy's safety. She was loved by so many that no one wanted to be the reason she was harmed."

"I was there." She slipped her hand into the front pocket of her jeans and Tex realized she was running her fingers over Lucy's coin. "Months after they mated, Dad and I were sent to pick up Lee's brother from the airport. We got back later because someone t-boned us on our drive home, slamming into the passenger side of Dad's truck. That's when I realized how bad things were. Lee didn't care that his brother was decapitated from the sheet metal that flew off the pickup truck that hit us. He was just angry we were late."

"I know." Thorn nodded. "Dad and Lucy spent the rest of that night trying to calm Lee down. Even after Dad came home, he stayed in the living room watching Lee's place, terrified of what might be happening over there. You could have died and Lee couldn't have cared less."

"Dad got me out of the car and with the help of the first police officer on scene, they were able to get me into the alley so I could shift, allowing me to heal the internal bleeding and head wound. I had to leave some of my injuries to make the story plausible, but that saved my life. There was nothing we could do for Lee's brother, not that Dad even cared about him at the time."

"What does this have to do with the position?" Tex wasn't seeing the connection and as much as he'd have liked to allow them to reminisce, there wasn't a lot of time before he had to be back in Texas.

"Dad was hard to live with at times, especially when he and Mom fought, but there were times that he was unbelievable. The compassion he showed me that night as he calmed me was something I'll never forget. I was frozen from the sight of my own blood, unable to move to heal myself, but Dad forced me to shift. Otherwise, I'd have died." She took a step back, brushing against Tex's front as he brought his hand to rest at the small of her back. "That same compassion is within Tex. You saw it firsthand when I cut myself on that beer bottle. Lee never cared when Lucy was bleeding. There wasn't a drop of compassion in that man. Do you need more evidence that Tex is nothing like him?"

"Believing it and finding a way to stop worrying about you are two different things." He tipped his head toward Tex. "I want to believe you'll never hurt her, but after everything..."

"I get that. The shit you went through makes trusting anyone hard. If you commit to me, you'll know without a doubt that I could never hurt her. I've only known her a short time, but I'd give my life to keep her from ever shedding a tear or being hurt." Unable to stop himself any longer, he wrapped his hands around her waist and pulled her back so she was resting against the front of his body. "I want you as the Captain of her Guards because I trust you'll keep her safe. There's no one else who can keep her as safe as the two of us can. So, think about it and you can give us an answer in the morning."

"If you choose not to come to Texas, I wish you the best," Rhett added. "You've got talent and ability that others don't. If you test out for another Alpha, don't let your need to impress them overwhelm what you're doing. You allowed that to happen during the first session and if Tex hadn't seen something inside you, you might have been eliminated." He grabbed Carleen's suitcase and opened the door. "I really hope you consider the opportunity. It would be great having you as part of the team and I could use your help training future guards."

"Let's get some rest." Keep his arm around her waist, he led them toward the door, but before he reached it she paused and looked back at Thorn.

"Will you come for breakfast? I'll get up early and make sure I can get some of your favorite chocolate chip banana muffins from the kitchen."

"I'll be there." Thorn nodded, sending his shoulder length black hair into his face, but didn't look back at her. "Night, Car."

On the short walk over to his cabin, Tex wasn't certain what to make of

Thorn's stance. He wanted to protect Carleen, and as noble as that was, it was also misplaced. All he could do now was hope that something they'd said would knock enough sense into Thorn that his attitude would change and he'd take the position. He wasn't holding out hope, which meant he needed to find someone to protect Carleen and fast. The idea of returning to Texas the following day without an official Captain of her Guards made him uneasy. He wanted her protected, and unless Thorn came around, the only other person he trusted with her safety was Rhett. It would cost him and Ben, but he had no doubt Ben would agree with the idea of Rhett standing in temporarily as her Captain.

Chapter Fourteen

The heat of Texas was just as Carleen expected, but the rest was nothing like she imagined. The wide open space made it appear as if it continued forever. There was something peaceful about the place. Ranches scattered along the drive to Manetka Resort drew her attention. The number of cows, horses, and other farm animals was overwhelming, making her wonder if there were more animals than people in the state.

"We're almost there." Tex slipped his arm around her shoulders, bringing her back against his side. "Ben has assembled the clan in the conference room. We'll meet with the clan and introduce you and the new members. Then I'll show you around."

"You don't have to. I'm sure you have things to do before your appointment." Her stomach tightened with anxiety at the thought of meeting the clan.

"Tad and Ben are going to deal with that."

"You should—"

"Don't, peaches." He pressed his lips to her temple. "It's an airplane, that's all. As long as it gets us safely from place to place, I don't care about any of the other details. The features aren't important to me. I trust them to get us a good deal on the plane."

"Since you're a licensed pilot now, don't you want to take it out for a test flight?"

"I trust them," he repeated. "I'd rather be with you."

"You're buying a plane?" Thorn turned in the passenger seat to look back at them.

"It will make it easier for us to get back and forth from Alaska without having to wait for one of the Brown brothers to fly in for us," Tex explained. "Rhett and I both have a pilot's license, and Ben is in the process of obtaining his now. In the future, I'd like to have an additional guard become a licensed pilot. This will allow them to play dual roles whenever any of us need to leave Texas. Taking a pilot who is a risk during a mission could leave a team stranded."

"I didn't even think to ask, but this plane you're going to look at is why Tad, Milo, and Courtney are staying? I figured Tad would fly you back, but I didn't realize Milo and Courtney would be coming as well."

"Tad knows planes and offered to look over whatever I considered purchasing. He also suggested that maybe Courtney should visit. Since she's human and most of the clan haven't been around many, it will give them a chance to adjust to the different scent. As her mates, Tad and Milo wouldn't allow her to be alone. Tad needed to check out the plane, so Milo came as well. Having the trio here will be a good test run for when the resort opens."

"Opening week, we've kept the number of reservations small, slowly building each week," Rhett explained, pulling the SUV up to the front of the resort. "It will give everyone time to adjust to it being open again. Plus, with the limited guards and staff, we can only handle so much. We'll work on building the team and with the new attractions coming soon; we'll be a whole new resort by the end of the year. Hopefully back at full capacity, too."

"I spent most of the plane ride here going over the information you gave me and I'd like to sit down with Barry as soon as possible." Thorn glanced out at the resort. "I want to get an idea of the floor plans so I know every possible escape route."

"You're acting like I'm in danger." She shifted in her seat as Rhett slid the gearstick into park. Last night she wasn't even sure Thorn would accept the position and had spent most of the night tossing and turning. It wasn't until he showed up at the cabin with his duffel bag in hand that she could relax. It was a complete turnaround for him and now he was fully committed to Tex, the clan, and her protection. He almost seemed back to his old self and appeared to be looking forward to the challenge in front of him.

"He's being a responsible Captain of your Guards." Tex lifted his arm from around her shoulders and took her hand into his. "If you haven't noticed, your safety is the most important thing to both of us. Until he gets the lay of the land and is ready, Rhett's going to be teaming with him."

"Leaving you unprotected? No." She stared at him, unwilling to believe he thought she'd be okay with this arrangement.

"At home I don't have guards."

"For the time being," Rhett interrupted. "When the resort is open, he will. We might not be hovering, but we'll be there. It's for his protection as well as the clan."

"The point is, I know my members. There's no reason to have guards shadowing my every move." He brought his other hand up to the side of her face and tucked her hair behind her ear. "I wanted you to arrive here as Alpha Female so they know where you stand from the moment we walk into that room. Still, after everything that has happened, they're going to be leery. Most of them have never been around anyone outside of the clan. They were kept in the tunnels, hidden away from the guests, because Avery was too afraid of what might happen."

"Even if you were going to a clan with less of a haunted past, you'd need protection. We don't know if any of Lee's supports will come after you as retaliation for Dad taking over the Mississippi Tigers. Killing you wouldn't just be a retaliation against Dad, but it would be a swipe at Tex and his clan," Thorn added. "So, no arguing. You do exactly what we tell you."

"You just had to give him the Captain of my Guards position, didn't you?" With a grin, she shook her head. "Let's go."

Tex chuckled and took hold of the door handle. "He'll protect you like I would and that's what you need."

Following Tex into the resort, she was so taken in by her new home that she was only faintly aware of the new guards and the trio from the Alaskan Tigers climbing out of the second SUV and falling into step behind them as they made their way inside. Entering the lobby, she quickly took in the space. Even with the ladders and other work equipment scattered around the room, the space was still large enough that people could relax there and mingle. The oversized furniture had been covered in plastic so it wouldn't be splashed while the walls were being painted. The floor-to-ceiling windows overlooked the massive swimming pool with several smaller hot tubs. Straight ahead was a reception desk, currently without anyone on duty. The outdoor fire pit made her do a double-take.

"I know you don't believe it, but we get a dusting of snow occasionally," Tex teased. "Actually, we added it because who doesn't love a good s'more? They're only really good if you roast the marshmallow over an open flame."

"Kids will love it." She glanced up at him. "I want a s'more now."

"Tonight we'll light it and have a celebration." He led her past the reception desk and down the hall toward conference room one. "You can have your s'more and we can mingle with the clan. It will be good for all of us."

"Is it wise to plan that when you're not sure how they're going to react to her? Not to mention me, Dawson, and Brody," Thorn said.

"I wouldn't risk her if it wasn't."

"We'll be here as well," Tad called from behind them.

"It will be nice to spend some time with Carleen and your clan before we leave. A relaxing visit," Courtney added. "I think a night of fun is what we all need. Bring on the s'mores."

"Ready?" Tex's voice was low as he squeezed her hand. Before she could answer, Rhett opened the door and Thorn grabbed hold of it, allowing Rhett to continue inside.

She wasn't sure she was ready, but since she was already mated to him, it was too late to back out. One last hurdle to jump and that was meeting the clan members. She could do this. After all, this was her home now. She knew that one day she and Thorn would find a new clan. She just never expected to be center of attention when she did. What if she wasn't cut out to be Alpha Female? The only benefit was that she wouldn't have to worry about anyone challenging her for the position. That wasn't how it worked. She was the Alpha's mate, making her Alpha Female. Nothing changed that.

Stop worrying. They're going to love you. Tex's voice echoed through her head.

This silent communication is freaky. Trying not to think about all the attention focused on her as they made their way toward the center stand where Ben was already waiting, she squeezed his hand. If their stares weren't enough to make her uneasy, the hushed whispers were.

Tex was amazed at the change within his mate. No one would have realized twenty minutes ago Carleen had been petrified as he led her onto the stage. Now all her anxiety was gone as she mingled with the clan members. She stayed close, touching him whenever she could, but she no longer had a death grip on his hand. Everyone was excited to have her there and she seemed to be returning the sentiment. More than that, she was at ease.

Watching her interacting with the members, he realized he had nothing to worry about. She was meant to be there with them.

"We need to talk," Ben whispered as they slipped from one group to another, welcoming Carleen to the family.

"Can it wait?" With his hand on the small of her back, he watched as one of their close advisors, Mario, neared them.

"You know I wouldn't ask if it could." Ben glanced around them. "It's waited too long already."

"We've got it covered," Rhett whispered from Tex's other side. "Thorn and I will stay with her."

"Go on. I'll be fine." Carleen glanced back at him. *Remember you trust them. I'm safe here. Your words.*

"I won't be far." With a break between greeters, he gave her a quick kiss. "Stay close to Rhett and Thorn. Tad and Milo are close by, too."

"Don't fret. My shadows will keep me safe." She shot him a cocky grin.

"I won't be far," he repeated as Rhett stepped in front of them, cutting Mario off, and giving them another private moment.

"So you said." Her hand slid down his chest as she leaned back out of his embrace. "Go take care of business. I've still got a lot of people to meet. Then I'd like a hot shower before the party tonight so maybe Rhett could show me to our place."

"I'll try to be back before then, so I can join you in that shower." Forcing himself to step back, he glanced at Thorn, quickly noting how her brother watched those moving about them. If it hadn't been for his connection as Thorn's Alpha, he wouldn't have been able to tell the Captain of her Guards was uneasy. Any aroma of uncertainty that most would give off, Thorn had been able to hide, allowing those around them to think he was oblivious to what was happening. It normally took years for a guard to develop that ability, yet Thorn was once again proving Tex made the right choice by giving him the position.

"If not, we can shower together later." She gave him a quick smile and turned back around to meet those who had made their way toward them. Placing her hand softly on Rhett's back, she let him know she was ready for Mario.

"Control room?" Without waiting for an answer, Ben started toward the staircase at the back of the room, leading up to a small chamber. Back when the resort had been at full capacity, the conference room was used for movie night and the control room had been the focus point of making sure everything ran smoothly. All the controls for the lights, projector, and sound were in that room.

Climbing the stairs, he thought back to the movie nights. He had never been there to watch a movie, but he remembered it clearly. It was loved by the children visiting the resorts and crowded on rainy days. The beanbag chairs and mats seemed to be a hit for the kids. He needed to bring it back. Movies for the adults hadn't gone over as well as it had with the children. There were too many other things the adults could entertain themselves with. Maybe he needed to turn the room, or one of the smaller conference rooms, into a full-time area for the kids. Eventually, clan children would be able to use it.

Closing the door behind him, he stepped toward the window overlooking the conference room below them. The moment he saw Carleen in the crowd, her guards and now Milo surrounding her, his concern dissipated. "Do we still have the beanbag chairs?"

"Most, yes. With all the painting and remodeling, they've been stored in a room down the hall. Why?"

"When you mentioned the control room, I started thinking about the movie nights. Maybe we should bring them back. We can discuss it later." He glanced over at his Lieutenant. "What's so urgent?"

"Do you remember Jamison? He stayed here a couple years ago with a friend of his."

"The lion and his friend Griffin. Wasn't he a black bear?"

"Yeah." Ben leaned back against the desk. "For the past twelve years, they served in the military together, and during that time they became close."

"I don't see what this has to do with the urgent matter at hand."

"Neither of them wanted to go their separate ways and neither Jamison's pride nor Griffin's sleuth would agree to the other joining. After almost six months of being on their own, they're missing the connection with other shifters and they reached out to me. They didn't figure a tiger clan would take them in, but they thought since the resort is about to open again we might be hiring. They've got skills we need and we've got something they need."

"Urgency fits how?" The annoyance in his tone wasn't something he even bothered trying to conceal. As Alpha, duty called at all hours and normally he didn't have a problem with it. Right then, he did. He didn't believe Carleen was in danger from any of the members, but his tiger wanted to be down there with her as she met the clan.

"Ty called after you left Alaska." Ben glanced out the window and down at the clan below. "It appears a small group of Lee's supports broke off from the Mississippi Tigers. Jack isn't sure what their intensions are, but they denounced him as their Alpha and left. They could be a threat to Carleen and Thorn."

"Fuck." Tex snarled. The thought of her being in danger enraged him.

"Jamison and Griffin can help protect her, the clan, and us. Even if it turns out that this group who left the Mississippi Tigers aren't a threat, Jamison and Griffin can train our guards in aspects Rhett might not be able to." He turned back to Tex. "These guys stopped Avery from attacking Julia."

"I remember." Tex didn't need to recall the hell that Avery put the clan through for that. That argument was one of the first times there had been a witness to Avery's rage from outside of the clan. He was pissed that a large party canceled their reservation and Julia, being on duty at the reception desk when it happened, received the brunt of it. All it took was one hit for Jamison to jump between them. "Where have they been for the last few months?"

"Bouncing around the states, seeing parts of the country they haven't before. After a scuffle that left a couple rogues dead, they're skipping their plans on visiting the Grand Cannon and getting out of Arizona before anyone else can find them."

He stood there weighing the benefits against the trouble they could be opening themselves up to by inviting these two into the clan. It wasn't just the lion pride or the black bear sleuth, but now that they had run-ins with the rogues, that was yet another possibility of trouble following the two. Still, what they had to offer could be worth it. "Have you discussed with them their willingness to commit?"

"I haven't yet. I wanted to speak with you before giving them hope, but I have no doubt they're interested."

"Make sure before you extend the invitation. I don't care how much they have to offer. Right now we can't afford to have anyone here full-time who's not committed to the clan. I need to know they're committed to what we stand for. They might not be desperate enough to commit to a tiger clan, even if it means being around their own kind through the resort." He watched as Mario continued to linger near Carleen, rising his tiger within. "If they'll commit, work it out with Tad and get them here."

"I have no doubt they'll commit and not out of desperation." Ben picked up a notepad from the desk and held it out to Tex. "I've spoken to them at length and their values line up with ours. Otherwise I wouldn't suggest bringing them here."

He read over the notes Ben scribbled on the pad and nodded. "Get it taken care of."

"One more thing." Ben glanced down at Carleen before turning back to Tex. "When you told me Thorn was going to be the Captain of Carleen's Guards, I had my doubts. It's unusual, but I can see he cares for her. He's a good choice."

"We'll need to determine where to assign Brody and Dawson. I have some thoughts on that, so we'll meet tomorrow morning with Rhett and go over things." Dropping the pad back on the table, he stepped to the door. "Dawson might be good for Captain of your Guards. He's good."

"Then you'll take Rhett?"

Tex shook his head. "For now, Rhett's assigned to Carleen. I want her safe. I can protect myself."

"Is it worth me arguing with you on that or should I wait until we sit down with Rhett tomorrow?" Ben shook his head. "Never mind. I'll wait."

"Save your strength for a battle you can win." Tex chuckled and grabbed hold of the door handle. "Going on your judgement, Jamison and Griffin might be the most help to us by leading the resort guards and handling security. I know Barry is handling the security under you, but he'd be more use to us as resort manager. This change would allow us both to focus on the clan. But let's wait until after I meet with them to make that decision."

"I agree. The clan needs the most of our attention." He tipped his head toward the window. "Go to your mate. I'll get things squared away with Jamison and Griffin."

"I'll send Tad up. Besides the appointment about the plane, I'm sure you won't have any issues arranging travel. At least on this end." Knowing his Lieutenant could handle that, he pulled the door open and headed down the steps to Carleen. As he made his way through the crowd toward her, he was no longer as relaxed as he had been. Only knowing some information wasn't enough for him; he needed to know what they were up against. Standing where he could keep an eye on Carleen, he pulled his cell phone from his pocket and opened his messages to text Ty. *How many left in Mississippi? Their plans?*

He didn't even have time to put his cell phone away before he got a reply. *Five. Maybe six. No threats made. Keep up your guard. Will call when we have more information.*

That did little to ease the concern tightening his muscles. His mate could be in danger from her former clan members. Five or six would be easy for them to take care of, but with his commitment to Tabitha, it wouldn't be hard to add to those numbers quickly.

"You're worrying your mate." Tad's voice pulled Tex out of his thoughts. "Turi and Trey are combing the shifter forum for a lead. Right now, there's nothing we can do but wait. I've already spoken with Ty. We'll stick around until we know if they're coming after her. He'll send more if she's in danger."

"Thanks, man. I appreciate it." He turned to the bear, not the least bit surprised to find Courtney at his side. "I actually need your help with something."

"Name it."

"There are two shifters who can provide substantial aid to the clan and our cause, but we need to retrieve them. I can't leave Carleen to go get them...not now." He tipped his head toward the staircase he'd descended minutes before. "Ben's upstairs. He can tell you more."

"Consider it handled." With his arm around Courtney's waist he headed toward the stairs.

With everything he could handle taken care of, he continued toward Carleen. His time away had given most of the clan time to introduce themselves, allowing them to slip away soon. Once they were upstairs, he could touch base with Jack and Ty again.

"Everything okay?" she whispered as he came up behind her.

"Better, now that I'm here with you." Placing his hands on her hips, he pulled her back against him. No doubt she felt what being near her was doing to him. "Let's get out of here."

"I haven't—"

"Tonight. Right now, I need you." He leaned down and kissed along the curve of her neck. "Unless you want to give them a show, let's go." With his arms around her waist he started moving her toward the door, giving her no choice.

"Tex..." Even as she called out to him, her body rocked back against him, humming with need.

"If I could have everyone's attention," Rhett hollered. "Carleen hasn't had a chance to meet everyone, but there will be time tonight..."

"Rhett understands and he'll handle things."

His announcement blended into the background as they made their way toward the door. It wasn't until they were out of the conference room and near the elevator that Tex turned back to Thorn and Milo. "Thorn, wait down here. Rhett will show you to your room and get you set up with Barry. Be at our suite at seven and we'll go to the barbeque. Milo, thank you."

"You know there's no need for that." Milo nodded. "We're family and we've got to watch out for each other."

He knew Milo was right. Finding the Alaskan Tigers had been the best thing that ever happened to him and to the clan. He was part of something bigger. "Tad and Courtney are in the control booth with Ben. I hear you're going to be sticking around for a bit, so make yourself at home. You know where you're staying on the tenth floor." The elevator doors opened.

"Go. We've got things under control. I'll make sure Brody and Dawson get settled as well." Milo gave them a knowing grin as the doors closed and the elevator started toward the top floor.

Every second in the elevator seemed like an eternity. Enjoying the way her body arched into his, he kept her firmly pressed against the front of him as he nipped and kissed along the curve of her neck. Moaning softly, she tried to twist so she could face him.

"Not yet."

"Please…" She begged breathlessly.

"For the next few hours, you're mine, peaches." Unable to wait, he scooped her into his arms and as the door slid open, he dashed down the hall to their suite. "It's shower time…"

Chapter Fifteen

Life in Texas was unbelievable and the unease that knotted Carleen's stomach since she first learned she was Tex's mate was gone. She had been nervous the clan wouldn't approve or accept her, but it turned out she had nothing to worry about. They had only been in Texas a few days, but everything had gone perfectly and she wasn't sure she'd ever felt more at home than she did there. This was where she belonged.

Enjoying her morning coffee, she stood on the patio near the pool as she looked out at the grounds. The construction crews were already busy on the second living quarters for the clan. The resort's suites were nice but once the clan began to produce children, they'd need more space. Before they could see an increase in their population, they needed to have more mated couples. Avery had done a number on the clan; even mated couples were limited.

Her gaze continued to scan the ground, pausing over each of the buildings that housed clan members. The sprawling building divided into apartments was at capacity and Tex had offered a couple of the resort's guest cottages for temporary use to anyone who wanted more space than they could offer in the resort. She glanced toward the only one that was occupied just as the front door opened. Ashley stepped out onto the porch, and in her arms she held her daughter, Nova. The adorable baby had her parents and the whole tribe wrapped around her finger. She was the first baby born in the clan's new beginning with Tex leading them, hence why Ashley chose the name Nova, meaning new.

"There you are." Tex strolled across the patio toward her. "I was wondering where you got off to while I was busy with Ben."

"I wanted some fresh air." She set her coffee mug on the railing and turned to him. "Did you get everything worked out with the security assignments?" Last night as he'd crashed into bed beside her, utterly exhausted, he told her they had almost everything worked out. Resort security was the only big aspect that remained. If the meeting was already over, she could only hope it meant he'd get a break. He'd spent most of the last two days working out everyone's new positions and selecting potential guards to begin training. Jamison, Griffin, Rhett, and Thorn would share the responsibility, giving the upcoming guards the best overall training they could get.

"Yeah, Jamison's the Director of Security Operations and Griffin, the Director of Security Response."

"Fancy titles, but it sounds like their jobs will overlap."

"Job titles make it official and with the resort about to open, we want the guests to be reassured we have security under control. They've worked as a team for years and just from watching them together, it's clear separating them would be disastrous. They'll work together to handle the guards and security for the resort. When the occasion arises that we need them on a mission or when we travel, they'll be available. Barry will step into the role of resort manager, giving us more time to focus on the clan." He reached behind her, grabbed her coffee mug, and brought it to his lips, taking a long drink. "Damn, that's good."

"Some women would kill if their man stole their coffee," she teased, looping her arms loosely around his waist.

"To think I was planning on spending the day with my beautiful mate."

He set the mug aside and wrapped his arms around her. "Everyone deserves to let off a little steam, so tonight that's just what we're going to do. Mario's making the best barbeque you'll ever eat, Barry's making Texas chili, and the kitchen staff is making more food than everyone can handle. We got lucky with Courtney and her mates still being here, because she's an amazing baker. She didn't want to be in the kitchen staff's way, so she took over one of the cottages with Milo. I'm not sure what they're baking, but I know we're going to have a delicious spread of desserts. We're going to gather in the dining hall, eat, drink, and celebrate."

"What are we celebrating?"

"Good news, the purchase of the airplane, being alive, and everything." He lowered his head, bringing his mouth next to her ear. "Jack called. Those who left the clan are not a threat to you; they never were. They wanted a fresh start and believe leaving Mississippi was the only way to get it. They didn't support Lee, but they're not sure they support Tabitha either. Right now, they're informing themselves on Tabitha's beliefs and determining where they stand before making a decision on a new clan."

"Everything's fine with Dad? Why didn't he call me?"

"Overthinking it, peaches." He leaned back to look at her, but kept his arms around her. "He's fine. Knowing you wouldn't tell him the truth, he called me to make sure you were adjusting well to the clan. He wanted to make sure you were happy."

"Tex?" a soft female voice called from behind them.

"Bree, come join us."

Tex stepped back from Carleen, giving her a view of the other woman. Seeing her shoulder length auburn hair and jade green eyes, it was clear she was Rhett's sister. Bree was the woman Tex spoke about when he pulled the glass out of her hand. Just thinking about her brought the images of Bree's cuts to the forefront of Carleen's thoughts. Each time she cut herself, it was to release the pain within her, to feel alive, never out of the desire to die.

"Actually, I um…" Bree shifted from foot to foot. "Rhett…he wanted…"

"Briallen." Tex stepped out of the embrace and went to the other woman. "It's fine. Rhett told you about Carleen. There's no need to be shy."

"I've been hoping to meet you." Carleen took a step closer, but then decided it was better to let Bree come to her rather than scaring her away.

"To see the freak of the clan?" Bree took a step away from Tex, but he grabbed her arm to stop her.

"You're not a freak." Knowing Tex wasn't going to let her run off, she closed the distance between them. "I know you nearly died, but now you're getting the help you need. Robin's been working with you and the whole clan has been supportive. You started talking to Robin because Rhett pushed for it. He was terrified that next time he wouldn't get to you in time to save you, but you're doing it for you now. I know there are times when it feels like you're alone, but you're not. Come, let's talk. We'll go into the library."

"The library."

"I know it's your favorite place. It's quiet and no one will bother us." She tipped her head to the side and raised her eyebrow at Bree. "You think I'm doing this out of pity, but you couldn't be more wrong. I'm not sure why, because I've screwed up enough in the past, but I think I can help."

"Touch her." Tex let go of Bree's arm and stepped away so he wasn't interfering with the connection he encouraged between them. "Bree, you'll know she's not doing this out of pity."

Carleen placed her hand on her forearm and let the connection between them flow free, allowing Bree to see the offer genuine. She understood why Bree had turned to cutting to ease the pain. There were many times when she had wanted something to ease her own pain. While cutting might never have worked for her, there were other options.

Alcohol had been restricted within the Mississippi Tigers compound, but when she was seventeen she snuck out see a guy she met with her Dad at the construction job. They went to a party where she ended up getting drunk. The relief she found in those few hours was unlike anything she experienced before. She'd have turned to it after Lucy's mating, to ease her guilt, but it was unavailable to her.

Everyone handled stress differently. Bree cut herself. Thorn let his frustrations out in the gym. She had shut down, hiding in her room. But since she left Mississippi that had changed. She didn't feel overcome with stress. Even now as the Alpha Female, she didn't feel overwhelmed. If anything, she thrived off it.

"I see." Bree stepped back, breaking the connection. "I think we'll be good friends, but right now I must get back to Rhett. He just wanted me to tell you Jinx agreed. He'll bring Summer and Claire for a short visit the week before the resort opens."

"That's great. Can you make sure Ben knows? I'll inform Ashley and Michael." Tex shot Carleen a grin. "Claire can test out the new play area in conference room three. That's where we decided to move the movie night to."

"How about lunch?" Bree asked before moving away. "I mean, if you're not busy."

"Lunch is great. How about I grab it from the kitchen and we eat in my suite?" She tipped her head toward Tex. "He'll be checking on the construction and remodeling, like he does every day at that time."

"Great. I'll see you there." With a smile on her face, Bree strolled back to the main building.

"I thought we'd spend the day together to make up for the lack of attention, and you go brushing me off." Tex kept a straight face, but the link between them gave him away only a split-second before the smile tugged up the corners of his lips. "Don't look at me that way."

"What do you mean?" She grabbed the front of his shirt and pulled him to her. "Maybe I should drop my shields and show you just how I'm planning to spend the next few hours."

"How's that?"

"Upstairs." She jumped up, wrapping her legs around his waist and her arms around his neck. "I want you."

"What am I, your sexual plaything?" His hands cupped her ass, holding her against him.

"Don't play like you don't want this." She snatched his cowboy hat off his head and put it on her own. "We've both spent the last few days focused on the clan. You in meetings, getting things lined up, and me getting to know the members, as well as getting to know the resort. I learned that Manetka is the Polish word for shifter, and I know we're going to make this a safe haven for our kind again. It's starting to feel like home. Right now, I don't care about any of that. I just want to feel you. Feel your naked body pressed against mine, your manhood buried deep inside me until I scream your name. Tex, I need you."

"Mate, you always have me." Holding her wrapped around his body, he walked toward the elevator.

Mate. She'd never wanted to be mated to an Elder, but Tex was different. He was everything she wanted in a man and more. The power and authority that rolled off his body didn't scare her as it had at first. Now it excited her. "I love you, Tex."

"Shit, Carleen." When they stepped into the elevator, he pressed her against the wall. "I've been waiting for you to say those words. I could feel your emotions, but it's not the same things as hearing it."

"I love you." Before he could say anything, she pressed her lips to his, claiming his mouth. She hoped the elevator would make it to the tenth floor before they lost control of themselves. It had been too long and their beasts were too demanding. They weren't going to last long. Once, the thought of someone finding them in the elevator might have bothered her. Now, she wasn't worried. She just wanted him. Her mate.

Preview: Furever Mated

Complete Crimson Hollow Box Set

Romancing the Fox

Sinopa refuses to live among the tribe and produce cubs, but to appease her family she agrees to Garret Fox posing as her fiancé for a week. The ploy backfires when an undeniable attraction manifests between her and the predator. Is he meant to be her mate, or is her life in danger?

Loving the Bears

Ari and Kaden always knew they'd share one mate who would complete their unique bond, but when they find Camellia—the right woman to satisfy them *and* their bears—they must help her overcome her past before she can accept the truth.

A Lion's Chance

After a near death experience, Ginger Fox takes off to visit her brother, who recently mated with the Deputy of the Crimson Hollow Tribe. Meanwhile, Liam O'Neil catches Ginger's scent and he can't stop himself. With the help of a little boy who needs them, Ginger soon realizes there's more to life than touring the country, but is she ready to settle down with a lion?

Swift Move

When the tribe sends Brett Oaks to bring home the runaway Swift, he has no idea she is his mate. Now he has to overcome her terror and need for revenge before he can claim her as his own.

Purrable Lion

When Captain Noah Jones, is sent to investigate recent attack near the tribe he expects to find carnage—just like with previous attacks. What he doesn't expect is to find *her*, his mate. Karri Mallory not only finds herself in the wrong place at the wrong time, but if she wants to stay alive she must put her trust in the very people The Saviors are hunting.

Bearly Alive

Jase, Chief of the Crimson Hollow Tribe, has stood aside, watching Becky deal with the demons of her past while and open her heart to shifters—but when his bear alerts him to the peril she's in, it's time to intervene and protect his mate. He must claim her now or risk his bear going rogue to eliminate the threats to her and her son.

Saved by a Lion

With a bounty on her head Arlene Mallory wants revenge but before she can get it The Saviors find her. Chained in a cellar she vows to take the information she has to her grave and it will be a painful journey. Roger is tasked with finding her, but he's doing it for more than his tribe—she's his mate. Will he find her before it's too late?

Marissa Dobson

Born and raised in the Pittsburgh, Pennsylvania area, Marissa Dobson now resides about an hour from Washington, D.C. She's a lady who likes to keep busy, and is always busy doing something. With two different college degrees, she believes you're never done learning.

Being the first daughter to an avid reader, this gave her the advantage of learning to read at a young age. Since learning to read she has always had her nose in a book. It wasn't until she was a teenager that she started writing down the stories she came up with.

Marissa is blessed with a wonderful supportive husband, Thomas. He's her other half and allows her to stay home and pursue her writing. He puts up with all her quirks and listens to her brainstorm in the middle of the night.

Her writing buddy Pup Cameron, a cocker spaniel, who is always around to listen to her bounce ideas off him. He might not be able to answer, but he's helpful in his own ways.

She loves to hear from readers so send her an email at marissa@marissadobson.com or visit her online at http://www.marissadobson.com.

Other Books by Marissa Dobson

Alaskan Tigers:

Tiger Time

The Tiger's Heart

Tigress for Two

Night with a Tiger

Trusting a Tiger

Alaskan Tigers Box Set Volume 1

Jinx's Mate

Two for Protection

Bearing Secrets

Tiger Tracks

Healing the Clan

Alaskan Tigers Box Set Volume 2

Her Black Tiger

Tiger Trouble

Alpha Claimed

Forever Creek Shifters:

Forever's Fight

Protecting Forever

Crimson Hollow:

Romancing the Fox

Loving the Bears

A Lion's Chance

Swift Move

Purrable Lion

Bearly Alive

Saved by a Lion

Furever Mated Box Set

Reaper:

A Touch of Death

SEALed for You:

Ace in the Hole

Explosive Passion

Operation Family

Marine for You:

Lucky Chance

Back from Hell

A Marine's Second Chance

Tanner Cycles:

Until Sydney

Phantom Security:

Different Sides

Undercover Agent

Cedar Grove Medical:

Hope's Toy Chest

Destiny's Wish

Leena's Dream

Fate Series:

Snowy Fate

Sarah's Fate

Mason's Fate

As Fate Would Have It

Half Moon Harbor Resort:

Learning to Live

Learning What Love Is

Her Cowboy's Heart

Half Moon Harbor Resort Vol. 1

United Homefront Ranch:

Destination Forever

Stormkin:

Storm Queen

Beyond Monogamy:

Theirs to Treasure

Clearwater:

Winterbloom

Unexpected Forever

Losing to Win

Christmas Countdown

The Surrogate

Clearwater Romance Volume One

Small Town Doctor

Stand Alone:

SEALed Rescue

SEALed in Texas

Through Smoke

Starting Over

Secret Valentine

Restoring Love